Cam

Lancelot's Redemption

by

Robert W. Hickey

Bill Nichols

Edited by Bill Love

Published by Robert W. Hickey

Camelot Forever

created by

Robert W. Hickey

Camelot Forever Lancelot's Redemption
copyright and trademarked 2021 Bobby Hickey.
All Rights Reserved.

Camelot Forever: Snowflake
copyright 2021 Bobby Hickey
All Rights Reserved.

Camelot Forever logo is ™ 2021 Bobby Hickey.

Chapter One

A beekeeper.

Not the most illustrious of careers, one must admit, but when introduced anywhere, the likelihood of being fawned over as that Mr. Holmes decreased drastically. From there, the detective could go about his business.

Falling beneath the radar, as it were.

That was where he preferred to be these days, quite honestly. The puzzle of the world was so much larger than it had been over 100 years before. So many things to discover, even now.

So many more mysteries to solve.

Some large, some small.

Some personal.

Such was the case of his great-granddaughter Elizabeth. Since the day she was born, she had been a continuing delightful mystery to observe and mentor.

And love.

He chuckled at the thought of the great consulting detective being a doting great-grandfather. Oh, not in the bouncing on his knee variety. No, that was more Watson's forte.

Holmes prided himself on being more the mentor type. Elizabeth was a part of his legacy. A great part, in his opinion. And in truth, that might also have been due to her ancestry from another lineage.

Before this business of using DNA to trace one's ancestry, Holmes had done a fair amount of research on the subject.

Interesting indeed.

And if she and Lawrence continued their project, what other answers might they find?

As well as what other mysteries?

Very interesting.

Ah, but he was but a humble beekeeper with no time for such endeavors. No. Of course not, he thought as he patted a stack of folders and files. Looking around his study, he realized it might be high time to install more bookshelves for a little light reading.

Soon, he would be welcoming another generation in.

Chapter Two

"I definitely felt a kick that time," he said, touching her stomach.

Elizabeth said, "Every time you kiss me."

"Please, my love, take it easy today." he said.

Lawrence Ban kissed his wife goodbye. He hated that she wasn't accompanying him to work at the university where he could keep her close, just in case. Not today. Not in her condition.

As important as their project would be, the upcoming birth of their first child was far more important.

And in any case, her own work was a good twenty minutes in the other direction.

"I have no idea what you are referring to, sir," she said, grabbing him by the lapel of his tweed jacket and pulling him in for one last kiss.

"Hm, so you say," he said, sneaking in one last peck on the cheek. He was all-too-well aware of the adventures she had had in the past, especially given her infamous great-grandfather.

Even though he knew she wasn't due for another two weeks and showed no signs of going into labor anytime in the immediate future, he joked as he walked to the car that this could be the day!

Fortunately, he was far enough out of her line-of-fire to not be beaned in the back of the head. She had quite the aim, that one.

He waved and settled into the forty-five-minute drive to his work. Many mornings he wished they lived closer to the college, but the cottage was exactly what they were looking for when they decided to leave their apartment and begin to start a family.

Not thinking it might happen this fast, he had been taken aback when one evening only weeks after the move, Elizabeth brought out a baby cake decorated half-pink and half-baby blue for dessert.

Overjoyed, the couple celebrated with cake and some sparkling ginger ale in champagne flutes they had on hand.

Lawrence reached down and put in one of his favorite cd's, Meat Loaf's Bat Out of Hell.

Chapter Three

Elizabeth watched the taillights of their car as Lawrence drove out of sight. Even for just the day, she would miss that handsome face.

"Pretty boy," she said, fondly touching his picture. If he had been nearby, she wouldn't have said it. Definitely not a nickname he liked much.

I'm not your pet budgie, Elizabeth.

Still, the name fits.

The little one, boy or girl, would be lucky to favor him. Of course, he would often say the exact thing about her.

She ran her hand over the soccer ball-size bundle of joy-to-soon-appear and smiled. How she wished her aunt could have been there.

And her parents.

She shook her head to try to shake away the memories, the tears, and the regrets. Uncle John would be coming round soon, and he would take one look at her face and know.

He might not be the world's only consulting detective like her grandfather, but he had his moments. It took a special sort of person to deal with the things he had, as well as the adventures. And well, including her grandfather. Sometimes, one might wonder if he was showing genuine human emotion or conducting some experiment in the human experience.

He loved her, of that she had no doubt, but the other thoughts were there. An inquisitive mind was definitely hardwired into her DNA.

DNA. There it was the focus of her life's work. There are many factors to consider, so many possibilities, so much promise.

What had its beginnings in an essay in school about one's family had become so much more. Had Mrs. Ptarmigan not handed her the essay marked with a failing grade and disparaging remarks about it being pure fiction, who knew what other avenue her curiosity would have followed? Write the truth, she had said, smacking the desk with her wooden ruler.

Ah, the look on Mrs. Ptarmigan's face when she presented what amounted to a book with footnotes, reference material, and copies of family photos followed by a special pair of guests who presented an inscribed copy of Sir Arthur Conan Doyle's accounts of their adventures for the school's library.

Precious.

And the course for her future studies was set into motion, using her own family line as a starting point. Degrees in science, history, literature and more helped to pave the way for the Big Project.

And that led to meeting the love of her life.

Oof. The little one was most definitely kicking. Perhaps it was her thoughts of love associated with Lawrence that spurred those football matches in her stomach.

"The other great love of my life, little one," she said, rubbing her belly.

Oof.

"Again, so soon?" Deep breaths.

Breathe.

Grab the phone.

Oof.

Chapter Four

He was thinking about what kind of scone would be best with his coffee from the Walking Cow Espresso shop. It was one of the bright spots for him in the little town of Winging halfway between home and the college. He had just enough time to try their drive thru and still make it to his class in plenty of time. Blueberry, perhaps?

Suddenly, as he was about to make the turn his phone rang. Elizabeth's ringtone. Before he could ask if everything was alright, all he could hear was "IT'S TIME... GET BACK HERE...NOW".

He turned around but to do so, he had to make a complete circuit of the parking lot to head back the way he had come.

Blueberry scones could wait for another day! His wife needed him!

Chapter Five

Camelot. The Past.

Snap.

"What was that?"

"Calm yourself, Arik. I told you before there are noises in the woods at night aplenty. T'is just some animal on the hunt."

"A bear, m'lord?"

"If it is, we would have heard more than just a twig snapping in the night, I would say. And stop calling me m'lord. Lancelot is fine."

The younger man looked at the knight with a touch of horror. "Oh, no no no, sire. I could never. I am but a lowly... nothing! While you are a noble knight of the king's Round Table! I couldn't!"

Lancelot held his hand up for the other to stop talking. "Arik, I am merely a man, that's all."

Arik tried to stop him from saying more. "No, m'lord, pardon me for saying so, but you are so much more! You are a legend among men!"

Lancelot laughed. "Look around you, Arik. Is this the life of a legend, traveling around the countryside, dealing with feudal lords and the evils men do, sleeping on the ground as would any man?"

"But you fought a dragon."

"No."

"You bested a giant!"

"Just a very tall brigand."

"You were raised by the Lady of the Lake!"

"Well, that one is true."

It was true, in fact. She had found him at the edge of the lake, lost or abandoned, and raised him. It was from her that he had received his sword Mundbora. It was said to possess some small magic. Perhaps it did, but magic was unreliable. Lancelot had long ago learned to rely on his own talents and skills as a fighter and knight.

And being a rather handsome man had not hurt matters, either.

Perhaps that had been what first attracted Elaine to him. Or perhaps it was his skill with a sword. Maybe it was just his smile.Whatever the start, from that union came Galahad.

Ah, Galahad.

Lancelot looked over at his companion who was still talking excitedly, occasionally eyeing the forest for a bear or a wolf or whatever his fears were telling him was out there. If only that companion had been Galahad.

Certainly, their relationship as father and son was well on its way to being mended, even if it was more from the son's efforts than his own. Pangs of guilt kept Lancelot at bay many times from being the kind of father he had wished for growing up himself.

Guilt.

He had plenty of that still. This debacle with Arthur and Guinevere was another reason to be away from the gossip of the court.

Arthur was his best friend. Gwen his second best. And Arthur's wife. And that was all the gossips needed to start trouble with their innuendo and cutting remarks.

Arthur's sister surely contributed her fair share of those as well.

The witch.

Perhaps it was unfair of him to call her such names.

No.

Witch definitely suited her.

If she was a witch, what did that make her spawn, Mordred? Well, there were words that described him as well. Lancelot had pitied the boy at times with his scrawny build and having Morgana for a mother.

Mordred's spiteful actions over time had more than killed that notion. Always underfoot and causing trouble...

Snap.

Arik's eyes darted back and forth. "Animal?"

Lancelot's answer was to slowly reach for the handle of his sword Mundbora while eyeing the woods in the direction of the sound. Arik took that as a cue to touch his dagger, just in case he needed to cut something.

The horses tied up nearby were suddenly restless, their hooves pawing at the ground, snorting. The packs, including several bags meant for some project of Merlin's, had been taken off and hung from a strong branch, away from any critters that might have ventured into the camp in search of food.

Around the campsite the night sounds of birds and bugs seemed to die down as the two focused, something in the shrubs nearby.

Suddenly, movement!

A rabbit ran out of the bushes, straight through their camp and disappeared into the night.

Arik giggled in spite of himself. "I should have caught that hare for dinner!"

However, he stopped when he realized Lancelot had not yet let down his guard. "Sire?"

"Shh."

"But-"

"A rabbit would not have made that much noise!"

From out of the shadows, a dark figure launched toward the knight. His sword flashed out of its scabbard and he impaled the thing as it descended upon where he had been sitting. In his other hand was his own dagger, which he used to stab the thing as it fell past him.

It landed heavily but struggled to rise. Lancelot kicked it over and pointed the tip of his sword at its throat.

Some foul creature it was that glared angrily up at Lancelot. Its skin was murky and mottled as if rotting. The stench of the thing would have alerted them if it had not been downwind.

"Who are you?" Lancelot demanded to know. "What are you?"

The thing hissed and gibbered, trying to find escape from the tip of Lancelot's blade.

"Can you speak?"

The thing opened its mouth as if to say something, revealing a mouthful of jagged rotting teeth. If the stink of the thing's body was bad, its breath was worse.

"Well?"

Its eyes, yellow and bloodshot, looked from Lancelot to Arik. Arik, who had stifled a scream at the attack, pointed his own dagger at the thing.

"Speak, creature!" he said. "When Sir Lancelot of the Knights of the Round Table commands, you will do as he orders!"

At the mention of the knight's name, the thing shifted his glare to Lancelot alone.

"Lansssselot…" it hissed.

Lancelot tapped its pointed chin with the sword and said, "So, you can speak!"

"You will diiiiiiiie…" it replied.

"A very limited vocabulary, I warrant, if not a bit boring. What is your purpose here?"

"Kill the knight."

"Yes, well, we've established that bit, "Arik said, finding a bit more courage with the thing pinned to the ground by the threat of being impaled once again. Its wounds oozed some vile ichor that might have been blood if not for the blackish, yellowish stains adding to it's unearthly nature. The thing glared and hissed at Arik, who fell back away in spite of himself.

Lancelot nudged the thing, "Answer me!"

Arik said to Lancelot, "Is it a demon? It's no man."

"Arik, that's what I'm trying to find out."

"You don't think it's after the bags you have for Merlin, do you? He's been said to cavort with the otherworldly."

"Arik, shut up," Lancelot commanded but it was too late. The thing's glare shifted to the packs hanging from the trees behind them near the horses.

"But-" Arik started to say before a screeching shriek erupted from the bushes and another thing jumped out. This time Arik did let out a scream.

The second creature, as disgusting as the first, loped across the campsite and launched itself at the suspended packs, frightening the horses in the process.

With a flick of his arm, Lancelot threw his dagger across the campsite into the leaping thing's back.

Lancelot's mount reared and kicked at the thing as it flailed about, striking it in the head. As it fell, it clawed at the pack, raking it with ragged rips. The thing fell to the ground, staring up as the contents inside spilled upon its face.

"Dirt?" was the thing's last thought as the hooves of the horse trampled it into the ground.

The first creature used the distraction of the attack to bat Mundbora aside and attacked Arik, who was leaning in far too close.

It landed on top of him, and he tried to stab it with his dagger. If only the knife wasn't pinned between them that might have worked, but Arik was no match for the deceptively strong creature.

Its breath reeked as it grinned with evil intent, its fetid stench coming out of the gaps in the rotted mess. It licked its lips with a tongue dripping slobber like a grotesque slug.It clawed at his collar and exposed his neck. As it reared its head to take a great big bite from the exposed flesh, Arik struggled to bring his dagger up in time.

Suddenly, the creature shook, and a blade sprouted from its mouth like a second tongue. If the thing wasn't dead before, it was now as it fell upon Arik, who finally managed to get his dagger up and pierce its chest.

It landed heavily upon him, and he could only lay there, not able to convince his muscles to work and push the thing off him.

Lancelot grabbed the thing by the neck and tossed it aside.

Arik lay on the ground, stunned, and covered with the creature's blood. Lancelot towered above him, concerned.

"Are you hurt? Did it wound you?" he asked.

"Um, no, I was just... um, resting. Covered in whatever that thing bled."

"Well, then," Lancelot said, offering his hand, "Your respite is over for now. We need to pack up and get back to Camelot. Arthur will want to know of this. And I'm sure Merlin will be quite interested as well."

They gathered up their gear, Lancelot taking great care to repair the sack meant for Merlin as best he could.

There wasn't much to save of the creature trampled by the horse, but they formed a litter from some branches and threw it on with the other. There wasn't any way Lancelot was going to even try carrying them on the horses the way they reacted to the things. Perhaps it was the smell, or that they could simply tell how wrong the things were to even exist.

As he finished packing, Arik said, "When we get back to Camelot, could I be the one to tell this story?"

Lancelot smiled and said, "Well, surely you've earned that. Be my guest."

Arik tried wiping off some more of the ichor, and after a bit, said, "Can I say it was three demons?"

Lancelot laughed, "How about four?"

They finished packing and made ready to travel. Arik put the last of the campfire out with dirt. They were once again in darkness, save for the faint light of the night's moon.

And in that darkness, Arik asked, "Oh, and uh, could we leave out the part where I screamed?"

Chapter Six

Elizabeth was at the front door holding her Uncle John's arm when Lawrence swerved into the driveway, nearly taking out a section of the picket fence.

John carefully guided her down the steps and into Lawrence's arms as he rushed to meet them.

"I got here just a bit early for our scheduled luncheon and found her doubled over trying to make it to the phone."

"I could have made it."

"Of course, you could. John, grab her getaway bag just inside the front closet."

"Right-o!"

"I told her I could take her to the hospital, and you could just meet us there," John said as he came back bag-in-hand just as they made it to the gate.

"I know, Uncle, but we had discussed that we both wanted to be a part of every step together," Lawrence said.

"I already made a call to the hospital to let them know we were on the way, so we just have to get there."

"Aaaaaa!" Elizabeth groaned out.

"And quickly!" John came to her side and asked, "What can I do, my dear?"

"Less talky, more walky!"

"Yes, yes, of course!"

Lawrence helped Elizabeth as gently as he could into the passenger seat of her car. John dropped the getaway bag into the back, next to the baby seat already buckled in.

Lawrence started the car and Elizabeth rolled down the window as John came around to her side and took her hand.

"It will be alright, my dear."

"Follow us in your car in case this turns out to be a false alarm, Uncle."

He squeezed her hand gently. "It's my considered medical opinion that this is no false alarm. Drive carefully, son, you have the two most important people in the world in this vehicle," he said before heading to his car. Then suddenly, he turned back and gave him a smile.

"Well, actually, three."

'I will, Uncle," Lawrence answered as he put the car in gear.

The hospital wasn't that far a drive, but Elizabeth's labor pains continued to increase at a rapid pace causing Lawrence to think they might have to stop and deliver the baby right there on the side of the road.

There was as much of a top surgeon that ever worked in a hospital right behind him. It could be done.

He said it out loud jokingly, but Elizabeth instantly threatened to make him have the next one if he did.

She said, "You will be the only other person apart from the doctors and nurses in the room with me when it happens." That put a smile on his face.

She continued, "Are we clear about thaaaaaaa-!"

He considered himself a strong person, but Elizabeth was even stronger, no question. There was no way he could imagine, much less endure, the pain she was going through.

He found himself looking forward to raising children with her and giving them a stable home. Unlike the many foster homes he had been in as a child, moving from one to the next, never finding the one where he felt as if he truly belonged.

Their child would have that, he swore.

Pulling into the hospital they were ushered immediately into the birthing ward. John was busy trying to convince Elizabeth that he could help and supervise the doctors, but she assured him that everything would be okay. If anything happened, he would be among the first to know.

The nurses pushed Lawrence and John out of the room, so they could prepare her. Lawrence was instructed to wait, and he would soon be brought back in when she was ready.

In the room, she was tucked into her bed and the nurses left the room. The doctor had come in and had done her spinal block. She had been told that there was no way she could have a natural birth.

As another contraction hit, they agreed with her that would be best.

The way that her hips were she would have lost the baby and most likely herself back in the days before cesarean birth. She and Lawrence both agreed that no matter what, they must do what was best for the baby.

A doctor walked into the room. Dressed all in white with his face covered, all she could see was his eyes. No charts. No clipboard. No stethoscope. He was leaning heavily on a cane. Those piercing eyes. A tall man, someone she instantly recognized.

"Hello, Grandfather," She said.

"That's Great-great Grandfather." He replied.

"Can we please just leave it at Grandfather?" she snapped back, the spinal block doing little for her mood at the moment.

"Yes, of course. We can leave it any way you want, great-great granddaughter." He took her hand and squeezed gently to reassure her. She squeezed back not-so-gently as another contraction hit.

"Sorry."

"No need, my girl." Under the face mask she could tell he was smiling.

This was the first time she had seen him in person since the night he and Uncle John saved her and her aunt.

As a child she was unable to understand why. Years later her uncle sat her down and explained that holding back the Stygian Knight who had attacked her and her aunt Anne, using the charms at his disposal, had physically taken a toll and that he was recovering from the punishment. Fighting magic with magic could take its toll on anyone. And the great detective was no different.

Knowing about the DNA project she and Lawrence were both working on, he had reached out to offer encouragement and advice on the project. Sometimes, they chatted almost daily, finding more and more things in common while discussing methods of proceeding in the research. She was also certain he was keeping tabs on her through John.

In one of those conversations, he shared the fact he might possibly have found a place that worked like her snowflake charm, a dead zone that could possibly hide anyone in need of being hidden because of their heritage, specifically their bloodline. Once he investigated more, he would share with her what he discovered once the little one arrived.

And he was sure her daughter would keep them busy for the foreseeable future.

"Grandfather, we don't know the sex of the baby." Elizabeth said.

"Hmmm, yes, well we'll see, won't we?" was his reply.

The door opened, and Lawrence walked into the room. The man in a doctor's gown gave her a wink and whispered, "Take care, little snowflake". He turned to leave, patting Lawrence on the shoulder as he passed.

"Good luck, old chap."

Lawrence looked at him and then back at Elizabeth who was smiling ear to ear.

Down the corridor, John Watson was never one to sit around in a waiting room. He paced the hallway. Sat and tried to read some magazines. Paced some more. And when he could no longer stand it, he strode up to the nurse's station and asked them what the blazes was happening with his niece. Just then, a limping man in a doctor's gown tapped him on the shoulder with his cane.

"How can I help you?" John said

"First, you need to stop pestering these fine ladies and allow them to do their jobs," the doctor said. "Then follow me."

"Hmmm." John said as he did exactly as the man said and followed him into the waiting room.

"So, just how long have you been here, Holmes?" John said.

"Not long, old friend. I happened to need some new beehives and the best builder of beehives is in the next town over."

"Beehives, eh," John said questioningly.

"But of course." Holmes replied, pulling his mask down. From beneath his robes, he pulled out his pipe and tobacco.

Watson put his hand up and almost smacked Holmes on the wrist. "Put that away, man. You can't smoke in a hospital."

"Ah, for the good old days, eh, Watson?"

"What?"

"The days when you could just strike a match and light up anywhere?"

"Are you mad?"

"Why, no, although there was that one case when I had to pretend to be, remember? Case of the Mad Hatter or something, wasn't it? Or have I confused that with the toxic waste adventure? The Case of the Hazmatter? Seriously, Watson, those titles..."

"What does that have to do with this?"

"Not a blessed thing, Watson. Except the fact that we managed to overcome all obstacles and triumph in the end."

"And?"

"And we shall get through this as well."

"Oh...well, yes. Of course."

"Took your mind off things just for a moment, eh?"

"...yes."

"Success!"

"Why, Holmes, I'd say you were almost in a jubilant mood, if I didn't know you better."

"You know me as well as most, even Moriarty."

"Well, thanks for that, at least."

"You know what I mean, old friend. There are not many people in this old world I would allow to be this close to me. Fewer still that I would call a friend."

"Hm."

"Far fewer that I would call family."

"Hm. Well. I should think so after all this time."

"So?"

"Did you see her?"

"Yes, and she looks well. Considering."

"What do you mean? Considering what?"

"We have found out that the bloodlines of the knights have crossed over and over throughout history. but never these two in particular."

John just looked at him. "Are you worried that the witch is going to finally come out of her nest?"

"No, not at the moment. Although I do worry about her son, as we should all." Holmes continued. "We don't know just how magic works but there's definitely something special about Elizabeth and Lawrence. And now the odds are greater that whatever is special about them will be passed down to their children."

"When the baby is born you have to get them to the cottage as soon as possible. It's a safe zone for those of the Round Table bloodlines and will do for now. I may have found a much larger piece of land that could house hundreds if not thousands. I'll keep you informed. But for now, keep my granddaughter safe."

"She's my niece also, you old codger, no matter if she's of my blood or not. Who do you think has looked out for her over the past ten plus years?"

"Her aunt. At least until she could do so no longer. You? You let her get married. And now this baby."

"Seriously, Holmes, have you ever tried to stop her from doing something that she wanted to do? Having an inquisitive mind is not the only thing she has inherited from you. Bullheadedness. She's a lot like you in that department."

A small smile appeared on his face. "I prefer to think of it as determined. And perhaps you're correct in that, my old friend."

Holmes turned and walked away. "I need to pick up my beehives. Just watch out for them all."

"Beehives, my fanny."

"Language, Watson."

"Hmph," was the reply as he watched Holmes's limp away, peeling off the doctor's garb and tossing it onto a gurney.

Watson considered snatching it up and using it himself when Holmes turned the corner, but he took no more than a step when Holmes stepped back into view.

Holmes knew his friend all too well…

So, he walked back and took the gown and mask back up. He might still have a need for it.

"Hmph," Watson said, turning on his heel and heading back to the nurses' station. The nerve. "Her aunt watched over her, Watson, not you. Not you, who never missed a birthday or school function. No."

"Sir?"

Watson continued grumbling. "I'm quite certain it was her aunt who patched her up when she skinned her knee. I'm certain-"

"Sir?" A nurse touched his arm, jolting him out of his melancholy.

"Sorry. Lost in my thoughts. And it's Doctor, actually."

"I'm sorry, doctor. Is there anything I can get you?"

"No, no…" I'll just wait.

Everything went as normal as possible except for the oddest thing: a power surge just as Elizabeth gave birth to a healthy baby girl.

The lights dimmed, flickered once and then were back up, followed by Angela's first cries in a whole new world.

No one appeared to notice one less doctor in the room, the one with a cane.

As the nurse lay the baby in the nursery, Watson's face was pressed against the glass trying to see the little one...a girl!

They named her Angela! And she was such a little angel. How fitting.

Oh, joyous tidings!

He looked over his shoulder, expecting to see William straining for a view himself. But no William.

Just to be certain, he chanced a look over the other shoulder as well. No Holmes there, either. Ah, well, he would be missing out on seeing this bundle of joy.

In her room, an exhausted Elizabeth was napping when he managed to look in. Her eyes opened slightly and a serene smile brightened her lovely face.

"Uncle."

"She's beautiful, my child." He quickly pulled out a handkerchief to dab away his tears. "Forgive me."

Elizabeth held out her hand to take his. "There's nothing to forgive, Uncle John."

"It's just that she reminds me so much of you when you were born."

"I was there, too, don't forget. Although I can't say I recall the details," she joked.

He chuckled. "I suppose not. Remind me one of these days then to share with you my writings about it."

"I would love that. You should start writing again, you know."

"Tsk, my writing is for another age. And the adventures of your grandfather and myself are hardly the page-turners they once were."

'Perhaps a romance novel?" she joked.

"Perhaps. If one could find a suitable companion for an old doctor of my years."

"Your years? Then you might try a museum."

He erupted in laughter at that. For all she had endured, she still had her sense of humor, bless her.

A day later, once the baby was checked out by the doctors and Elizabeth was ready, the hospital allowed for mother and daughter to leave.

"After the doctors allow you to go home, I'll be by in a couple days to check on you and baby Angela." said John as he leaned over and gave Elizabeth a kiss on the cheek. "It's vitally important you go straight home."

"Yes, Uncle, straight home."

"And remember:.."

"Keep the snowflake on when I leave the house." Elizabeth said. John looked at her as if it shouldn't have even been a question. She hooked her thumb on the chain of her necklace. "You should have heard the nurses when they tried to take it from me."

"Well, they obviously had no idea who it was they were dealing with, eh?"

John smiled and exited the room just as Lawrence came in. Having heard that last bit, Lawrence looked at her and started to say something, but Elizabeth cut him off... "Don't ask if you really don't want to know or to believe."

He took his wife's hand and kissed it. "I just wanted to say thank you."

She cocked a tired eyebrow. "Oh?"

He smiles, "Thank you for granting me the gift of being a father. And for the gift of having my own family. This is the second-most special day of my life."

"The first being..?" she asked.

"You're the detective's granddaughter. You'll parse it out, I'm sure. Now, rest."

"Then kiss me, my pretty boy, and let me sleep."

"Perchance to dream?"

"Ah, well, that part already came true."

Chapter Seven

Camelot The Past

"Where is he?"

"And hail to you, too, Kay."

"Oh, welcome back, Lancelot," the large man grumbled. "What happened to your man? Is he ill? And what is that smell?"

"Adventures on the road, I fear. Now, you were looking for someone?"

"That devil-spawn imp, Mordred."

"And what did he do this time?"

"Never mind. I aim to find him and teach him a lesson. Now, forgive me, I really can't stand the stink. Burn those clothes and whatever that is your horse is dragging."

The large knight stalked off in search of Mordred. Only then did Lancelot get a look at a patch of scalp on the back of Kay's head that should have been covered by hair.

He laughed and continued on his way. Arik looked back and forth as he realized the instant someone passing caught wind of the stench coming from them.

For most of the morning Lancelot had been met with such greetings from peasants, passers-by as well as the occasional soldier and knight as he made his way to the castle of the King of the Britons, his friend, Arthur.

Although he had been away for many weeks traveling, all knew the knight by sight and by reputation.

Not by smell, though, as the stench from the pair and the litter being pulled behind one of the horses reached them.

Often upon his return people reached out to Lancelot upon horseback just to say they had touched one of the bravest of the Round Table. Some would hand him food, some cups of water, and some even flowers woven into rings which he looped around his arms.

This trip, they just threw flowers, from a safe distance.

Through hard times and good over the past years, Arthur and his Knights of the Round Table had brought much peace to the land, along with justice and a look to a brighter future.

Today was one of the days where that did not matter enough to overlook the smell...

Around him the local folk far enough away went about their lives, smiling and waving. Any moment he thought they might even burst into song.

Peaceful though these times were, Lancelot found himself pondering whether there was still a place for him in all that peace.

But then, who knew what adventures the future held?

Ah, blessed adventure. He would take that any day over one laden with needless drama.

"Weary traveler, have you lost your way?"

Speaking of...

"Good morning to you, Morgana," he sighed.

"Odd. You don't seem all that delighted to see me upon your return to merry old Camelot. And you seem...ill-prepared to be received by your King. Do you not respect the proper dress and etiquette demanded by the royal court?"

Down a stone stairway stepped the sister of his king. Morgana. Beautiful and yet not. There was something of her that did not seem...right.

"You misjudge me, milady, I am but weary and filthy from a long journey across the lands of Britain and am eager to see the king, your brother, before I rest."

Morgana smiled. Surely, she was trying to appear friendly and concerned for the knight of the Round Table who had earned his way into the heart of her brother as his closest friend, but there was something behind that smile, something intangible.

Something dangerous.

It was well-known that while she was a lady of the court, she had ambitions beyond simply being someone's wife and mother. She followed Merlin around Camelot, flirting and flattering, eager to know the secrets of his magicks.

The old fox, though, had merely taught her minor tricks. She could make smoke come out of her ears, although many said that was no trick but a mere side-effect of her temper.

"Of course," she said, "That must be it. How did your travels fare? Did anything interesting happen? Slay any dragons, did you?" She cast an eye at the litter behind the horse. Arik averted his eyes to avoid her gaze and meandered around to the other side of the horses away from the couple in conversation.

"No, lady, no dragons. Only monsters in the skins of men and...other things."

She leaned forward and said, "Truly? You must tell me more! Were they...demons, by chance? I have heard such things roam the night, looking for the souls of innocent men?"

Arik tried not to utter a noise, but a sound like eep might have escaped him. He clamped both hands over his mouth just to be certain.

"I meant only that the evil men do make them more of a monster than any fabled dragon."

"Pity," she said, disappointed.

"Yes, it's tragic that with all the good in the world, there is still a darkness intent on dimming the light."

"Actually, I meant: Pity that you only limit your scope to the providence of men," she said, obviously done with the conversation and walking off.

Well, at least, that encounter was over. He was ready for some rest but first he would need to see Arthur.

And Guinevere.

Oh, and Merlin. The list was a long one.

Odd that Morgana never once acknowledged the smell that permeated the air around them...yes, odd that...

"Ow."

Something bounced off his head. An acorn. Then another, followed by muffled giggling behind a nearby tree.

"Ha ha."

"Mordred."

A thin, gangly youth peered around the trunk of a nearby oak, a cruel little grin curling the corners of his mouth up into his sunken cheeks.

"Mordred, if you wanted to get my attention, you needed only to call my name. And besides, Kay is looking for you."

"This is a lot more fun, sir knight, than pestering that big oaf," the boy said, rattling acorns in the palm of his hand. The way he said "sir knight" sounded as if it was supposed to be an insult.

"Well, you have a surprisingly good aim for one so well-hidden."

"You would be surprised where all I can hide, sir knight. Sometimes in plain sight!"

"Yes, well, I must be off to see the king."

"Tell me a story first."

"Mordred, I don't have the time. Find me later after I've had some rest and something to eat."

"Now."

"Mordred…"

In an instant, the look on the youth's face changed from pleading for a story to be told to fury at being put off until later. So much like his mother. Or possibly his father, whoever that was. Morgana kept that secret to herself.

"I want a story now!" Mordred screamed and flung another acorn at the knight who caught it midair.

"Mordred, I've only just returned to Camelot. I'm tired and hungry and I have things to do for the realm and the king before I rest."

"The realm? The realm? Who cares about any of that? And to the devil with the king!"

At that, Lancelot launched the acorn he had caught back at Mordred and plunked the boy squarely between the eyes.

"Ow! That hurt! You could have blinded me!"

"I hit what I intended. Learn some respect for your king and your elders."

"Oh, yeah? This is what I think of my elders!" Mordred said, picking up a rock and flinging it at the knight as hard as he could.

Again, Lancelot caught the missile midair, much to Mordred's surprise. Lancelot smiled and tossed the stone casually into the air as if testing its heft. Surprise turned to horror and Mordred quickly covered his forehead with his hands and made a mad dash away.

The sting of the rock hitting his backside made him all the faster. His hands quickly moved to cover that target. That Lancelot had only the one stone probably didn't occur to him at the time...

Lancelot laughed at the fleeing youth, caring little at the moment for whatever drama Morgana would feign at the indignity paid to her offspring, the nephew of the king.

"You will pay for that, I fear."

"It was worth it, I assure you, Merlin!" Lancelot smiled as he turned to the figure behind him standing amongst the foliage, looking for all the world as if he was having a conversation with a small tree.

Perhaps he was.

"You've been away for far too long, Lancelot."

"Why, Merlin, did you miss me?"

"Doubtful. I knew where you were. At least where you were supposed to be. Did you bring them?"

"I believe you tasked me with this favor before I left and I promised I would do it."

"Actually, I tasked all the knights before they left to patrol the length and breadth of the land."

"You wound me. And here I believed I was the only one to whom you had entrusted this mighty task."

"Did you truly?"

"No, of course not. Gathering a bagful of dirt from each place I visited is hardly a mighty thing to ask. And besides, Galahad told me you asked him for the same favor, as did other knights."

"Yes, well, now that you've obviously found out you were not my favored errand boy, hand them over."

Lancelot called to Arik, "Bring the bag meant for Merlin. The younger man reached into his travel pouch and pulled out a bag containing the samples of dirt Merlin had asked him to fetch.

"Here you are, wizard."

Merlin inspected the parcel and its contents. "It's been ripped."

"An unfortunate mishap with something in the night. I brought you extra gifts," Lancelot said, indicating the litter.

"So I smelled," Merlin said, crossing to the litter and pulling back the covering. "Oh, look, two heads! That is interesting…"

"Actually, it's two creatures. One was rather messy."

"Damn, a two-headed thing would have been far more interesting, but nevertheless, an unexpected surprise."

"Is it?"

"What do you mean?"

"You always know more than most. You know what these things truly are, don't you?"

"I might. Although I had hoped to be wrong. For once."

"Well?"

"Tales for a later time, sir knight. Now, have your man bring them to my tower along with my bag. And try not to damage it further, boy," the mage commanded.

"Who, me?" Arik said, peering over the saddle, trying not to be noticed.

"Yes, you. Now, come along. And don't burn those clothes yet, either. I can use that dried ichor. You just never know when you might have a need."

Lancelot nodded to Arik to accommodate the mage. He turned to Merlin and said,

"So, why do you need all this dirt?"

Merlin looked at the knight and said, "Mud pies."

"Not funny."

"Oh, dear. And I've been trying to improve my wit. I find people will open up to you more if you make them laugh."

"Since when do you care about people, mage?"

Merlin again gave a quiet look, then said, "You would be surprised."

"Definitely."

"Now, my dirt. You followed my instructions?

"And your directions. I covered the area as you requested."

"And you said the words with each one?"

"Exactly as you instructed."

"At least someone listens. That oaf Kay quite nearly ruined the whole thing, mixing up two simple words."

"Really?"

"No, not really. I had already Kay-proofed the incantation."

"So, it was an incantation. You told me it was a blessing over the land."

"It was, in its own way. So, you see, I Lancelot-proofed it as well," the wizard replied, beaming. "Spell, blessing. It is beyond me how you see the two things as being any different."

"You are a strange one, Merlin,"

The wizard walked away to claim his prize and said over his shoulder, "You have no idea."

Lancelot called after him, "When will I get to see what you're using the dirt for?"

"How about when Hell freezes over? Is that a good time for you?" Merlin muttered.

"What did you say?"

"Um...Next spring! Can only be done in springtime"

"Hm."

"Just curious, but were you having a conversation with that tree as we approached?"

"Hm, That tree? No, no of course not. The one next to it. Why, yes. Why do you ask?"

"It isn't something you see every day."

'Well, perhaps you should. Shall I introduce you? I call him Oaky."

"You gave him a name?"

"Oh, yes, there is great power in names. And he likes it well enough, I suppose, having a name. He claims one day he shall grow a face! Won't that be something?"

"Indeed, a strange one, Merlin."

"Be off with you. I have dirt to sort."

So, that was one visit off Lancelot's agenda. Realizing that not all of Morgana's advice was ill given he decided to clean up and change into fresh clothing after sending his filthy garments to Merlin. He found Arthur in the Great Hall that housed the fabled Round Table, surrounded by several of the other knights who hailed Lancelot upon his entrance.

Arthur came to greet his friend and clasped him by the shoulders.

"Lancelot! We wondered when we would see your return!"

Lancelot looked at his friend and king. "Arthur, you've known I was in Camelot before the first girl in town smiled and waved my way."

That brought a great laugh from the king, "True!"

"And if not that, then I'm sure Mordred would have come running."

"Mordred? Why?"

"ARTHUR!"

The scream tore through the hall and reverberated off the walls. Several of the gathered knights headed off in the opposite direction of where Morgana erupted, dragging Mordred behind her. Kay turned away. Dealing with that woman...

"Ah, Morgana, always a delight."

"Shut it, Arthur, I am angry."

"Really? Whatever could be the matter? Not enough clouds in the sky to make the day dark and dismal? Not enough blight in the harvest to starve a few of the country folk?"

"No, that ruffian there assaulted my child, your nephew! Just look at the lump on his forehead!" She pushed the boy up to the king for scrutiny, jabbing at the lump with her own finger as she pointed it out. "Look at it!"

Mordred, for his part, apparently would have loved to have been excused from any part of this conversation, preferring to stir the pot but reluctant to help clean up the mess afterwards.

Arthur gave the boy a solemn look. He leaned close to him to get a better look at the supposed injury. The boy looked everywhere else in the room except his uncle's eyes.

Arthur said, quietly, "And what, pray tell, caused such horrific damage to your noggin, boy? What lethal pellet assaulted your forehead with such deadly force?"

Mordred tried to look to his mother for support, but Arthur stopped him. "Mordred, a man answers with the truth. I would have no less from one of my knights or those who might someday be."

Mordred's eyes at once met Arthur's. "A knight?"

"Someday, Mordred. You are the nephew of the king, after all."

The boy straightened his shoulders and said, "It was an acorn, sire."

The room erupted in laughter.

Mordred stood, mortified. His cheeks flushed red as the laughter rocked the hall. The knot between his eyes reddened as well. Arthur raised his hand to quiet them, aware of the boy's humiliated state.

Galahad pointed to the bump, "Methinks he is growing a horn. Is he a mythical unicorn?"

Mordred fought back the tears as long as he could but failed at his task. He ran from the hall, stopping short of the doorway, and turned to shout, "I hate you all!" before disappearing into the depths of the castle.

That left the company of knights chuckling amongst themselves. Many of them had been the victim of the brat's taunts and tricks so there was little sympathy for him.

Arthur, though, wished otherwise. But for now, the damage was done. Perhaps he could find the youth later and make amends.

On the other hand, Morgana was having none of it. She stood clenching and unclenching her fists and began mumbling. To some it sounded more like a growl from some beast, they would say later.

Lancelot felt the hairs on his arms and neck stand on end as she stood, trembling in fury at the insult to her son. The knights stopped in their mirth and began to look alarmed.

He stepped forward and knelt before her, "Milady, my apologies for my affront to young Mordred."

The sudden gesture caught her off-guard and she fell silent. She stood among them for several uncomfortable seconds, then turned and stomped out of the hall.

The knights watched her go, saying nothing or not knowing what to say.

A hand landed on Lancelot's shoulder.

"Thank you, Lance."

"If I hadn't, I somehow doubt smoke coming out of her ears would have been the next thing to happen."

"She wouldn't dare, my friend. I am the king and her brother."

Lancelot stood and looked at his friend solemnly, "I hope not, Arthur."

As they joined the other knights now gathering around the table, trying to laugh off the past few moments, Lancelot looked in the direction of Morgana and Mordred's retreat and sighed.

"Somehow I fear for the future where they are concerned," he said in a low voice.

"What was that?" Arthur asked, turning back to him.

"Nothing to worry about."

At least for the present.

Chapter Eight

Holmes was once again at home, comfortable in his easy chair, enjoying the pipe Watson wouldn't let him light in the hospital.

The lights dimmed, flickered once and then were back up.

A granddaughter. Life and the line continued.

And to make certain of it, he would have to get to work ascertaining the feasibility of the magic safe zone.

Chapter Nine

She awoke.

Lying where she had crumpled in her apartments, the woman some deemed dark and terrible (and rightly so) struggled to utter anything more than some random mumbling. It could have been a spell but probably not...it sounded more like cursing. With a lot of expletives.

The room around her was decorated lavishly with items of antiquities. Not that she was enjoying the view much from her current vantage point. The last rays of sunlight shone through heavy drapes, particles of dust wafting in its rays. Outside, the balcony allowed for a view that could take in all of London.

Well, the better parts, anyway.

The woman crumpled on the floor had merely been crossing the room. Simple enough. Something she did all the time, in fact.

This time, though, she had been struck down halfway across right in the middle of concocting a bit of revenge magic against the local utility board. How dare they try to bill her twice the amount as was usual? The lights had dimmed, flickered one and then came back up.

A fleeting thought as she fell was that her cursed brother had finally arrived in this time period.

As her knee hit the opulent rug, the thought changed to the idea of something else, of something being born and a part of her being torn away. As it had just months ago.

Certainly, her balance was gone at that point, but a bit of the magic she tapped into was pulled away to...somewhere else. To someone else.

Merlin was her first guess as her hand reached the rug.

Not-Merlin was the conclusion as the hand proved useless in stopping her fall and slipped out from under her.

When her face bounced off the thick rug, she cursed whoever it was. The stinging of the rug burns would only fuel her rage.

Once she woke up.

Not trusting her legs just yet, she crawled across the room to reach the telephone. For the agony being inflicted upon her knees someone would pay.

Not being able to quite reach it, she pulled the phone off by the cord to crash heavily on the floor near her. Then she mustered the strength to click the receiver down to get a dial tone.

Buttons were pushed and soon it was ringing on the other end of the line.

"Find my son and send him to me now."

The voice on the other end said some things, obviously glad to be far away from her immediate reach.

"Now, Moog, or you will be the next volunteer to try out a bit of revenge magic I've been dreaming up. The very nasty kind."

She sat braced against the wall after she hung up. That is, if hung up meant just throwing the telephone off to the side.

It had taken her son years to fully recover from a battle where he had come across someone who had used counter magic relics to protect a child from her brother's bloodline.

In a tobacco shop, of all places.

Nearly killed, it had taken years of spells and sacrifices to heal him back enough to go hunt down her enemies once again.

She would have him find this aberration and eliminate it. Nothing and no one else would get in her way. And no one would stop her from killing her brother when he finally appeared.

The room was too warm but she didn't feel like crawling back to reach the curtains. So, she started an incantation and outside the clouds began to gather and obscure the dreaded sunshine.

Now, back to putting the utility board in its place.

Hm. The power company. She liked the sound of that. She grabbed the phone cord and pulled it to her again. She had a few calls to make.

Let it rain.

Chapter Ten

Six months later

It had rained all day.

With little end in sight, John Watson had put off going out until the last minute, hoping for an end to the dreary weather. But no, it was apparently not meant to be, according to the weather people on the telly.

In flipping channels, a news item caught his eye, one about the acquisition of a power company on the north side of London. Truly, he couldn't care less about the company and or about business in general. No, it was the person who had bought the company.

If, by person, one meant a vile demoness of a witch.

Or would that be witch of a demoness?

Morgana LeFay.

With his good friend William, he had run afoul of her and her associates several times over the years, the worst time over ten years before. The episode had almost killed his friend and had taken years for him to recover, even with all his magical healing trinkets and charms. Thankfully, he recovered and spent much of his time with his bees.

Running late, John hurried out of his terrace home on Burway Court. On the east side of Croydon just south of London, it was usually a quiet, cozy place where he could still do a bit of writing in between the odd adventure now and again.

Elizabeth kept after him to write a blog or some such. Once he found out what that actually was, perhaps he would do just that.

So, he was running late to meet his god-niece and her husband. That was not so unusual. At present, he seemed to have a thousand things to do and a thousand more to forget doing. Perhaps one of those blog thingamajigs would help him keep his thoughts and responsibilities on track.

Or perhaps he could simply just make a list? But a blog? What an intriguing and strange word...

What was he supposed to be doing?

Oh, yes. Elizabeth and Lawrence!

As he opened the door of his 1963 Rolls Royce, he happened to look down and see the front tire flat. Dash it all, that was a brand-new tire!

However, as he bent down to inspect it, he said aloud, "I'm too damned old to be changing a tire in this kind of weather."

Ah, well, as he managed to retrieve the spare from the trunk, he realized the rear tire was flat as well. Then he noticed it was not-so-much flat as shredded. Shoddy! This was a Rolls-Royce! The dealer would hear of this in a tersely worded letter from his solicitor.

And what was that odor? Sickening and vaguely familiar. Not in a good way.

Just then, he heard the sound of some animal moving in the trees nearby that bordered a small park.

Circling the car, his fears were confirmed. All four tires, shredded.

The thing in the trees might be something more than just some animal and suddenly seemed to come closer.

His hand went into his coat and clutched a small object in his vest pocket.

Suddenly, the noise stopped.

John stepped toward the door with as light a tread as he could manage, but so intent was his attention on whatever was in the woods, he missed the bottom step and stumbled into the front door.

And dropped the charm.

The noise started again, more frantic, coming closer. He picked it back up. And the direction of the noise seemed to shift, slowly, reluctantly, away from where he stood between the car and the house.

John fumbled for his keys, almost dropping the charm again, and barely managed to get the door open as he thought he saw something coming through the foliage.

He almost fell through the door seeking safety inside, then slammed the heavy oak door behind him. He backed away from the frosted glass as some shadowy figure approached the door. He fumbled his way into the hidden drawer of the grandfather clock and pulled out the service revolver he still kept on hand. He raised his revolver and aimed at where the thing's head should be as it moved back and forth, making a wheezing sound.

It was trying to smell him.

And there was that smell, oozing past the door through the keyhole and every gap in the facing, the smell of decay, of rot.

Of death.

He kept his revolver pointed at the door. The wood might hold but there were other protections William had insisted on incorporating in his friend's house. If only he could stop his hands from shaking…

But wait, what was it William had told him, had tried to drill into him as some surly sergeant back in the corps? Bullets wouldn't work against things such as this, but the charms…

He dropped the revolver and grabbed the charm, holding it out in front of him as he made his way to the light switch.

With his other hand he flipped on the front light. A raging hissss erupted from the shadow and suddenly, it retreated.

Reaching into his pocket, he pulled out a brand-new portable phone and slid the front cover up, revealing the keypad.

Trying to balance it all and dial didn't work so well, so he backed away from the front door and set the charm down on the table next to the bowl.

Once dialed, he snapped the charm up and held it to his ear while pointing the phone at the door. Then realized his mistake and switched.

If it had been the gun, William would no doubt have chosen that moment to quip that he always did shoot his mouth off and chuckle as he sauntered away.

Ringing.

Ringing.

Finally, "Holmes? Is that you? Yes, something most definitely is wrong. No, I haven't left my home yet. Yes, I know she was expecting me over an hour ago. Would you please stop for five seconds while I attempt to make sense of what just happened?"

He hurried through the events of the past minutes and paused to hear the response.

"No, no, I'm fine, just a bit ruffled at the moment. But the car, though, Four tires, four flats.

"Well, of course I had the charm right here in my pocket. Never mind, I'll just get a taxi and meet you. What do you mean we can't trust? Oh…yes, true."

"Fine, I'll wait for your driver. Within the hour. It will be fine. I'm sure Elizabeth will forgive the delay. Of course, I'll wait for him inside. Do you think I'm a madman, Holmes? Yes, I know the protection is stronger in the terrace house than outside. Can't be helped but Elizabeth is going to be upset… She needed my help with the little one."

"I know this isn't a good sign. This was an important speech for Lawrence. Yes, I know who his bloodline is and how…"

"Curse it, Holmes... I know..."

And so it went for several moments until the glow of headlights approaching shone through the frosted glass.

William's man was quickly at the door to escort him to the car. John paused at the Rolls, petting the car as he would a faithful hound. He touched a scratch in the paint.

No, scratches plural like claw marks. Down the entire length of the car.

Meanness.

Spite.

Evil.

Settling himself into the back seat of the car, he took his phone out to call Elizabeth. She needed to know he would be late, but he wondered if he should also give her a warning.

Danger was afoot.

Chapter Eleven

The Recent Past

On the docks of the River Thames, the situation was obviously not going to end well.

At least for the moment that was how it looked. The carefully planned attack on the Stygian Knight had not gone the way it had been laid out.

Other members of the squad lay scattered around the docks. Rowan couldn't be sure if they were even still breathing. He certainly hoped so, but if not, he was more than ready to take on the brute if he had to.

He just hoped he didn't have to.

And just in case, he still had his gun.

If only he had thought to bring a grenade launcher.

Thump.

Thump.

Thump.

Silhouetted against the harsh amber light of the next lamp post down, the hulking brute of the dreaded Stygian Knight of legend strode into the pool of light.

He wore no suit of armor, just a fine suit tailored to his large frame, a white one over a black shirt. No tie. And in his hand a blade.

A large, wicked two-handed thing close to the size of a Claymore.

It was probably a trick of the light that made it look as if it glowed.

The brute stood the blade on its tip and rested his hand on the pommel. And smiled cruelly.

"Is it only you left?" The brute was bigger than he realized this close.

"I wouldn't want to spoil the surprise, Mordred."

"Oh, good. So you do know who it is you are about to face in battle."

"A spoiled man-baby far past his expiration date."

"I'm no child, as you can surely see for yourself. Especially as I'm about to deliver you from your pitiful existence."

"Talk. Talk. Talk." Rowan hoped that by goading the brute, mistakes might be made in anger.

"Just for the record, which knight of the Round Table are you the little snot of?"

"Shut up and fight, Mordred."

Chapter Twelve

Hampton University north of Croydon.

It was a small lecture hall that could hold at capacity over five hundred people but currently had less than fifty with most of the attendees scattered throughout the first few rows.

Younger people, most likely students, occupied much of the first couple of rows while behind them the crowd were older and behind those older still. And apparently bored, as they continued to talk amongst themselves rather than listen much to the speaker. One bearded gentleman whom she knew to be the Vice-Chancellor of the school sat surrounded by a selection of the faculty known as his "court", although no one dared sit just next to him.

And off in the farthest corner, a lone figure with no one sitting anywhere close.

The speaker this rainy afternoon was Lawrence Ban, one of the younger professors at Hampton University and a specialist in DNA research.

Elizabeth's husband and father of the precious sleeping bundle on her shoulder.

So, Uncle John was going to be late for some reason. Saying that he had simply lost track of the time was so unlike him. No, there was something else, something he wasn't sharing, at least not yet.

Up on the stage, Lawrence had already begun his presentation. He said, "With our research, we have been able to trace back and find a person's entire genealogy provided there are genetic samples available."

Ohs and ahs came from the front rows while murmurs and mumbles came from those behind them.

"Even into medieval times," he added.

With that there were more of the same, but from the rear of the auditorium a derisive Hah.

Lawrence gave an irritated look to the obvious detractor but continued, "My wife Elizabeth, for example," pointing off to his left to a lady cooing at a small bundle of blankets on her shoulder.

With her husband's recognition of her, she managed a small wave and a nod to the attendees, then gave him a smile of encouragement.

Lawrence then continued, "Elizabeth has taken DNA research beyond anything we thought possible."

"At the same time, we have utilized the university's vast records of historical information as well as that from libraries, churches and other offices all across Britain to create a database of people, places and events that rivals few others."

"At this point, I should take a moment to thank a very dedicated team of students who have assisted greatly in this quest for knowledge." With that, he gestured to some of the younger folks in the front rows, much to their delight and pride at having contributed to such a project."

"Their work and enthusiasm have aided us mightily in constructing a timeline and model for our past." Behind him, a screen lit to show a map of Britain spotted with multi-colored dots.

"Each dot represents a small piece of that information. The colors each represent a different aspect of the database. We can zoom in on a person, a place and go from there to follow a family li-"

"Yes, yes, Professor Ban. We're quite aware how genealogy works, a voice came from the rear of the auditorium. Coincidentally perhaps, from the same direction as the earlier chortle. Everyone present was no doubt acquainted with the condensing tones of the Vice-Chancellor's voice.

"Can we raise the light a little, please?" Lawrence directed one of the students manning the tech boards. Time to deal with this thorn, he thought. Finally. "Now, Vice-Chancellor Justan, you were saying?"

The older man stood, smoothing out his long white and brown beard.

He rested his hands on a silver-tipped walking stick, a sneer evident.

"We are all here aware of the focus of your project, just as some of us are all-too-aware of the mounting costs attached. And for what? To glean from musty old books and records our family histories? I daresay it is not worth it, in my estimable opinion."

Then he paused, perhaps daring a rebuttal from any quarter of the room. Especially from the man standing at the lectern.

To his surprise, Lawrence smiled and asked, "Well, Vice-Chancellor, you might very well say that, but may I ask how far back you know your own family?"

The older man laughed and said, "The Justan family can trace its lineage back hundreds of years. My second great-grandfather was a captain in His Majesty's navy. He was knighted for his service."

The other gentlemen around all nodded and briefly applauded with a small chorus of "Here, here," and "Good show".

Vice-Chancellor Justan seemed to stand just a little taller and puffed out his chest. He was clearly winning in the exchange.

Lawrence continued to smile. "Quite something of which to be very proud, to be sure, but can you go back even farther?"

At that, the slightest of ruffles permeated the confidence of the older man, "Well, no. Family records were lost in a fire at some point before that."

The smile on Lawrence's face widened. "Really?" and he gestured at the screen. 'As you may recall, a few months ago, we asked a few key figures in the faculty if they would assist. And you were one of those most gracious to comply. Do you remember?"

"Of course, I'm not addle-minded, Professor Ban."

"Not saying you are. You'll be happy to know that our research did indeed show your ancestor. Jeffrey?" The student at the tech board tapped some buttons and the lights on the screen onstage dwindled to one.

"Now, that light is you, Vice-Chancellor. And we know that you were not born here and have lived elsewhere in your considerable lifetime."

The light on the screen became a line that traced a path over the map, finally stopping at a point just north of London.

"Adding in your direct family lines, your father and mother, their parents and so on, we see a more-complete picture of the Justans and the related families." More lines appeared on the map, spreading out in places like the roots of a tree.

When it stopped, Lawrence pointed to one dot in particular and said, "Here is your second great-grandfather."

"Now, knowing these facts will only take us so far, agreed? Now, we add in the DNA aspect of the equation."

At that, he knew he clearly had Vice-Chancellor Justan's attention. The older man appeared to lean forward on his walking stick, transfixed at the sight on the screen, holding his breath.

But Lawrence turned around and walked to the other side of the stage. "As I stated before, my wife Elizabeth has taken DNA research farther than it has gone before, tracing bloodlines of families. We theorize that we can even follow those lines back into medieval times, even back to the time of Camelot and the knights of the Round Table."

He paused.

"Or King Arthur himself."

"Balderdash, Ban. Do you truly expect us to believe you can trace the family of some figure from a folktale?"

"The answer would be sir...yes."

"That is fantasy, not science!"

"Vice-Chancellor, not only can we do it...we have done it. We call it the Snowflake Codex. Like a snowflake, no two histories are exactly the same."

With that, he turned to the screen and the map cleared with a wave of his hand. Actually, the student on the board followed his cue and made it happen. A bit theatric, perhaps, but the smile and nod Elizabeth gave him made him smile in return.

He continued, "Now, this," indicating the screen, "is my wife Elizabeth and her family bloodlines".

As before, lines on the screen blossomed out of the original point and wove their way back through time.

"This is her family tree, so to speak, with just the historical records. Now, we add in the DNA results."

The veins grew even more in a different color and finally stopped.

"And voila, we have a much more complete family history that reaches back through time to the years of the Round Table and beyond."

The response around the auditorium was varied, as Elizabeth had suspected it would be. From the excitement of the students to the disbelief of the faculty present.

And the figure in the far corner had apparently moved a couple of rows closer to the front.

Vice-Chancellor Justan grabbed up his walking stick and pointed it at the screen. "So, in lieu of actual science, how do you justify these findings, Ban, besides science fiction? Magic?"

Elizabeth watched the exchange and sighed. She and Lawrence had expected this very thing. And from this very person.

The Vice-Chancellor had opposed their project from the beginning, even to the point of hindering their requests for resources to further their records searches and other necessary steps to procure samples for the DNA aspect of the project.

It hadn't been easy, to be sure. Or made easier by him. Apparently, however, the Vice-Chancellor had not counted on sparring with the granddaughter of the world's foremost detective and where they were lacking in resources, they made up for it in other avenues of procuring what they needed.

The older man continued to shake his walking stick while Lawrence took it all in, nodding and almost smiling. So predictable.

And across the auditorium, the lone figure had moved closer by another couple of rows. Even though he had lessened the distance, there was still no seeing him clearly while wearing a rumpled Fedora and some ill-fitting clothes. Had it been in the winter, she might have chalked it up to someone just trying to stay warm. Or at least dry, given the rainy weather.

But there was something not quite right and eerily familiar about the figure. The way he seemed to test the air…and the closer he got to anyone else, apparently he must smell unpleasant. Several of the faculty gave him a disapproving look and a couple of them even moved a few seats away.

She wished Uncle John was here so he could take the baby while she investigated. This mystery needed to be solved...

Yes, she was indeed her grandfather's progeny.

Just then onstage, Lawrence had apparently reached the end of his patience with Justan's jabs now accompanied by a chorus of the emboldened faculty around him. Elizabeth hoped it would not lead to any rash actions. Her Lance was a slow burn but once it reached temperature...

"Not only, Vice-Chancellor, have we traced Elizabeth and other bloodlines back to the knights of the Round Table, but we have seen a pattern of those bloodlines being erased. As if by design!"

Oh no.

This was exactly what they had decided not to reveal. Not that it wasn't in their findings, but it could find itself in the wrong hands and more of the knights' bloodlines could be put in jeopardy.

The look of realization on her husband's face showed he knew what he had potentially just done. He looked at her and mouthed I'm sorry.

He tried to get the presentation back on track, "Even though our research was initially created to help discover if certain diseases and health issues were hereditary so they might be dealt with or looked for earlier, we've stumbled onto something that needs to be researched more. If it is true that someone else can discover and wipe out an entire family's bloodline, what does that bode for other families?

The Vice-Chancellor answered, "And to my mind, that question brings others to mind, such as how anyone else would accomplish such a thing. What science or magic would they be using? I would like to know how they might possibly be more advanced in gene research. Than you appear to be at this time, Professor Ban?"

Lawrence looked at the group of men and then over to his wife who had started pacing.

"Well, sir, that is something we intend to look into."

Instead of making the anticipated smarmy retort, the vice-chancellor merely nodded and said, "See to it that you do."

The presentation wrapped up quickly after that, much to both Lawrence and Elizabeth's surprise. Several of the younger attendees gathered around Lawrence to congratulate him on the presentation and ask questions.

The Vice-Chancellor stood at the rear exit and gave the gathering a long look before pushing the door open and leaving.

Elizabeth went to Lawrence and handed him the baby to a chorus of oohs and aahs at the beautiful child from the female contingent of the group. Lawrence began to ask what was the matter she made for the other side of the auditorium where the figure had been.

But he, whoever he might be, was nowhere to be seen. Smelling him, however, was another matter.

It was much like the smell of a... wet dog.

Chapter Thirteen

That morning

"What is this supposed to be, Gilbert?"

"It's a healthy nutritious breakfast, mum. I believe your son placed the order for you. There's a card if I'm not mistaken."

Morgana glared at him.

"To be frank, mum, he is quite the frightening individual."

"Where do you think he gets it?"

"A fair point, mum. I hadn't considered that."

"Well, here it is, Gilbert. I like you but I'm in a mood now so I'm going to curse you. Within the hour you will die. To anyone watching, it will look like it was your fault. Which it is, since it was you that brought me this healthy, nutritious breakfast."

Spell cast.

"B-beg pardon, mum?" Gilbert asked, blinking furiously.

"Never mind. Forget I said anything. That's also a curse, by the way. You'll never see it coming."

"Yes, mum. Will there be anything else?"

"Sausages. Coffee. Now."

"Yes, mum." he replied with a smile.

The main dining area of the Waterford that morning was awash in sunlight filtered through grand windows looking out over a sumptuous garden setting with flowers blooming and a fountain. It was a view many paid to enjoy on such a morning.

Morgana LeFay abhorred it, but she did enjoy the coffee. And sometimes the tarts.

Anyway, this was where her son wanted to meet and who was she to deny her offspring his fancy? No doubt there was the possibility of some mischief, perhaps a little mayhem, and that always made her day so much better.

Where was the scamp anyway? It was just like him to keep her waiting, even though he had set the time and the place.

Such an awful view. And such shoddy service to have brought her this, this-

Just then, she remembered something about a note and noticed the small envelope propped against the glass of orange juice, fresh-squeezed presumably.

Opening it, there was a card. Inside she managed to decipher the scrawled message. It was written in a hand she knew so well:

"Good morning, Mother. Enjoy your breakfast. Your living son, M."

She smiled as the waiter arrived to pour her coffee, looking somewhat antsy. Of course, the idea of presenting her with the exact opposite of what she desired would be just the sort of something her beloved son would do.

As if on cue, he appeared at the entrance of the dining room and sauntered past the help.

Mordred.

While she considered herself a beauty, her son was a large, chiseled brute of a man, more hunter in search of prey than a handsome man out to breakfast. The looks he received from those dining, some appreciative of the view, some envious, some apprehensive, some even fearful, made for a bouquet of reactions headier than any made from the loathful blossoms outside. He wore a pair of very expensive sunglasses that hid his eyes, but all present would have sworn he was looking at them.

She extended her hand and he bowed to kiss it, then sat in a chair that looked for all the world too small and too fragile to hold his massive frame.

He gestured to the repast in which she had neglected to indulge. "Not hungry?"

She gave him "The Look" mothers gave to petulant children at which he roared in laughter and proceeded to help himself by pulling the plates to him and digging in.

"I don't know what you think is so humorous. I could have poisoned it all, just for spite," she said, watching him wolf down the omelets made from the whites of the egg followed by the oatmeal.

"What?" he said, between bites, "And risk injury to this body? Hardly your style. Those kinds of spells take much out of you these days. Why labor for another?"

"Who says I would? Perhaps this time I would just let you suffer."

"Oh, would you now?" he said with that cruel smile of his as he shoved a spoonful of eggs in his mouth.

"And how was your meeting last evening?" she asked, sipping her coffee.

He stopped shoveling and grinned, his mouth a disgrace. "I dispatched a few of the opposition. Minor players, though, except perhaps for one. He slinked away somewhere to lick his wounds, methinks."

"So, you lost one is the upshot of your story? You couldn't finish the job?"

"He went into the sewers. I'm not going to follow him there."

"Hm."

"What's that supposed to mean?"

"Oh, nothing."

"I hate when you do that, Mother."

"I know."

Just then, the waiter brought a platter of assorted sausages, links, and patties, and placed it on a tray next to the table. Mordred helped himself to some links and then to coffee as well, heaping in a couple of teaspoons of sugar.

His mother watched as he slurped it down. "So much for your body being a temple."

"I deserve it."

"Do you, now?"

He shoved a sausage in his mouth and said, "On the upside, I believe I may be on the trail of DuLac."

Morgana bolted upright, nearly knocking over the carafe near her. "And you're just now telling me this?"

He grinned cruelly. "All in my own good time, Mother. You know that. Is there no gravy?"

"Wipe your mouth."

'Mother," he purred, "don't be such a...well, you. I wanted to tell you when I had more solid leads to follow."

"It has been a while since you managed to do any real damage to the bloodlines. Your adventures last evening don't really count, you understand."

He glared at her. "There are far fewer, thanks to me. And the rest of the vermin have gotten better at hiding. But not for long."

"Good."

"I have Moog and his hounds working on something more…and you will like it."

"Tell me."

"Not now. We are about to create some chaos that will flush them from hiding and I intend to enjoy my bit of fun. Then you can be about your business again, scheming away."

"Yes, scheming...shall I remind you where that scheming has gotten us? Wealth? Power? Immortality?"

"Yes, well, true immortality for you perhaps, while I must find a new host body when the old one gives out."

"What would you have had me do, Mordred, let you die?"

No answer at first, then "Sometimes I think you kept me alive for your sake more than mine."

"How dare you..."

"Oh yes, how I dare, Mother…"

"Lovely card, by the way. You misspelled "loving.""

He dragged the sleeve of his expensive suit across his mouth. wiping off the crumbs of his breakfast, glaring at his mother all the while.

"Did I?" Pushing himself away from the table, he took off the jacket and threw it onto the table.

"Take your jacket."

"Why? I'll just get another one, just like this body if I need to."

He stalked out of the restaurant, pushing past the few who didn't hustle themselves out of his way.

She watched him leave, making as dramatic an exit from the restaurant as his entrance. An elegant brute...

So far removed from the sickly child he had been. She blamed his father, what's-his-name, for such poor breeding stock. Sad that the rest of that family's line had met with such tragic ends...

Yes, so sad.

Mordred getting lost in some caves with his cousins had instilled that stupid fear in him. After that, he never visited his father's family again...or ventured into any cramped spaces.

It is ironic that his true body, preserved by magic, was safe in a place he would never venture. Safe from the hands of the progeny of those Round Table fools.

The lengths to which she had gone to in order to save his life.

There were times when she regretted making that deal.

But if she ever lost him...

There was a gasp from the other patrons of the restaurant, and someone screamed. Outside, Gilbert the waiter, while carrying a tray to a waiting table outside, had tripped and fallen headfirst into the fountain and apparently hit his head. Then subsequently drowned.

Simply tragic.

Morgana got a chuckle out of that for the rest of the day.

Chapter Fourteen

God had decided to cleanse the earth again by flood, or perhaps it was just another day in Merry Ol' England.

John missed the farm where he had spent years protecting and raising his god-niece with her aunt. The quiet life suited him more, it seemed. However, once Elizabeth started college and Ann passed, he decided to leave the farm and move closer to Elizabeth, so he could be close to her if needed.

He was forty-five minutes late. First, the delay because of the flat tires and the whatever-that-thing-was and then waiting for William's driver.

At first, he was willing to sit back and be driven but the man was too slow, too cautious, taking the long way to avoid any possible pursuit.

Five minutes into the trip, John left him on a corner with instructions to have the Rolls fixed. He had started to refuse but John was having none of it and the man simply nodded and pulled the car over to the curb.

William may like to be chauffeured around but John still preferred the thrill of driving. From the very beginning of the automobile, he had long enjoyed it.

And personally, he thought William might be the teensiest-bit afraid of it. One fender bender in Leeds and that was the last of it.

No, William tended to overthink it as he did with most things. Not everything had to be calculated out and triangulated before you reached the next intersection where there was a station wagon, a taxi and a lorry trying to figure out who went next.

John would just forge ahead!

That's it, old man. Talk a good game. He wasn't looking forward to seeing the disappointment in Elizabeth's eyes.

He had missed Lawrence's speech and wouldn't be able to help her with the little one, but he would sally forth, determined to do his best and protect them.

Whatever had shredded his tires was most likely trying to keep him from getting to Elizabeth and most likely didn't have the best intentions for them.

He hit the gas pedal a little harder and sped past a sedan, a taxi and a lorry waiting at an intersection.

Go.

Chapter Fifteen

It was such a simple task.

Pick Watson up at his home. Take him where he needs to go. Then do it in reverse.

Sigh.

Holmes' patience with his oldest living friend had been pushed to the edge many times. Of course, this was just another one of those times.

It wouldn't be the last, knowing Watson.

Sending his best man and car to pick John up and drive him to his granddaughter was just the start of it.

Now, his man was at Watson's terrace house waiting for a tow, having had to walk back there after being put out of the car.

The report of the car's condition was not a good one. It was at that point Watson should have stayed at home where it was safer.

But no. He still imagined himself a man of action these days in stark contrast to Holmes' days of discovery. And the keeping of bees.

"That damn fool," he mumbled as he walked between beehives. "He knows the witch will still be looking for her after all these years and now with that husband of hers and the baby, well, it only makes matters worse, doesn't it?"

The bees said nothing in return, they only buzzed and milled about their hives.

It had been over ten years since his battle with the creature on the streets of Old Brixton. It had taken every magi-relic at his disposal from his years traveling the world over and it had barely been enough to stop the demon spawn of Morgana.

Once he recovered from his physical injuries Holmes had spent the intervening years studying the magi-arts and researching appearances of the witch stretching back in history. He had to find out what she wanted and how to defeat her son.

Holmes had replenished his relics ten-fold but knew that the only way to defeat her was to wait for the arrival of her arch enemy, her brother.

And hopefully that arrival would herald the savior they needed to deal with the witch and her spawn for all time.

And Holmes could get back to his bees.

"Ow!"

Pulling out a drawer from a hive next to an old water well on the west side of his property, a bee had gotten into his glove and stung him on the wrist.

The bees on the west side were always a bit more temperamental. He must make a note of that.

"Damned bees" William said as he picked up his cane and continued to other hives removing drawers and draining them, careful not to get stung again.

Chapter Sixteen

That morning

Outside Waterford, his white Bentley was brought around by a valet who had apparently drawn the short straw to retrieve the large man's vehicle.

The young man drove the car as slowly as he could, hoping to avoid any mishap to his charge.

He should have balanced that fear with the one of not wanting to get under Mordred's skin by making him wait longer than he wanted.

Impatient, the big man growled and stalked to meet the slowly advancing car. Seeing the man approach unnerved the valet enough to cause him to hit the accelerator, making the car lurch forward directly at Mordred, who sidestepped out of the path of the Bentley.

Almost.

The tire ran over his foot.

The big man roared, and the horrified valet quickly lowered the window and began apologizing profusely.

'I'msorryI'msorryI'mso-"

He made it that far before Mordred grabbed him by the collar and pulled him out the window. Fortunately, the valet had neglected to buckle the safety belt but that was little consolation when he found himself almost nose-to-nose with the hulking man.

Near enough to smell what the man had just had for breakfast in the restaurant beyond, the valet could also smell the expensive cologne that oozed off the man, evidently in an effort to cover up a lack of a proper bath. And some other odor...

It reminded him of death somehow.

Mordred growled, "Be very thankful you are not of those I hunt, peasant. Otherwise, you would be gutted from here" he jagged a greasy finger in the valet's neck, "To here," he said, punching him in the stomach and tossed him onto the hood of the next car in line, shattering the windshield.

"Hey!"

"Do something. Please." Mordred challenged. Not getting a response or caring if there was one forthcoming, he sank behind the steering wheel, put it in gear and mashed down on the accelerator.

The older couple stepping out into the sunshine barely missed being hit as the Bentley peeled out of the valet parking line. One could imagine their surprise at nearly being run down one second just after seeing a waiter fall into the fountain and drown, then looking to see the other valets helping one of their number off the smashed windscreen of their automobile.

One of the valets shielded his eyes in the sun watching the car leave to get the license plate number.

It said MORDRD.

He turned to the others and said, "Was that a sword in his rear seat?"

Chapter Seventeen

After the presentation's conclusion, some of Lawrence's students had talked him into getting a cup of coffee at a nearby cafe they frequented to continue the discussion on DNA and the next steps in the project.

Elizabeth had agreed, provided it was only a few minutes and one cup of coffee. Both had to be at work the next day and the baby would probably be up in the middle of the night again as she had the past few months.

As they left the lecture, Elizabeth kept a watchful eye for any sign of the mysterious, smelly stranger. That was when she spotted vice-chancellor Justan off the main corridor as they were leaving the hall.

The older gentleman was paying far too much attention to one of those student bulletin boards touting guitar lessons and offering ride-shares home.

Leaving Lawrence to his gaggle of students, Elizabeth turned the baby stroller in the direction of the vice-chancellor.

"Vice-chancellor," she said.

"Oh. Mrs. Ban," he answered, pretending to be surprised and to be distracted from his surveying the landscape of the bulletin board.

"Thinking of taking up a musical instrument or getting a magazine subscription?"

The older man chuckled and said, "No, I was just trying to...uh...think of a way to talk to your husband in private after that most...illuminating presentation."

"Well, I'm afraid he'll be surrounded for a bit. Is there something I could help you with? He'll be inundated for a while, I suspect." Behind her, Lawrence was indeed surrounded by students, all trying to ask questions and make pithy comments, anything to impress the professor (and possibly score a rewarding research assignment).

"Um, yes."

"So, what was it you wanted to discuss?" In her stroller, the baby was cooing and reaching for Elizabeth.

"Yes, well, you may have noticed that I did not pursue the issue of my ancestry beyond what was already known."

"You did sort of let it go much quicker than I would have expected," she said as she picked up her little one, "Afraid of the answer, perhaps?" she said, smiling.

The vice-chancellor started to respond, then stopped himself and took a breath. Then answered, "Yes and No".

"Oh?"

"Yes, because for all these years my family has told and retold the story of our illustrious ancestor as if we were the ones who had fought those battles ourselves. Our pride was great."

"And no?"

"And no, because of the very real possibility that the generation before him might be pig farmers and serfs."

"There isn't anything wrong with being a pig farmer."

"No, I suppose not. However..."

Elizabeth put her hand up to stop him from continuing. "I completely understand, Vice-Chancellor. I do get it. It's one thing to have a legend in the family; it's quite another to possibly find that legend rooted in the mud. Hm?"

He chuckled, embarrassed. "You must think me incredibly vain, Mrs. Ban."

"Not at all. To be quite honest, that is a very valid concern. I myself had much the same thoughts, having a somewhat-legendary ancestor and God- Only-Knows who else dropping out of the family tree once it was shaken?"

"The idea, though, deserves exploring. Especially when it comes to the idea that someone may wish to use the Snowflake Codex to eliminate whole families."

At that, the vice-chancellor coughed. Loudly. Then he whispered, "I wasn't at all sure what to make of this. I received correspondence from someone who said he or she represented a party most interested in your research."

"Really? Any idea who?"

"No. Not precisely. The return address was that of a solicitor in London. That solicitor has only one client of note and that is a major power company."

"What would a power company want with the codex?"

"I don't know, but I thought it best to keep up the appearance of the old fuddy-duddy everyone seems to agree that I am."

"Hm, not sure that is the word most would use, sir."

"Trust me, I know several of them. We are not immune to a bit of graffiti in the men's washrooms."

"Trust ME, it isn't just the men's."

"I believe your husband is trying to leave."

Across the lobby, the gaggle of students and her husband had slowly traversed the distance to the door, only to be halted by one of the Professor's other critics seeking to throw his opinionated eggs into the basket and suggest that Lawrence not waste valuable lecture space with ridiculous assumptions.

As they made their way out the door, Lawrence started to again defend the project as he had already done on so many occasions with the faculty of the college.

Thankfully, the rain had let up for the time being.

Elizabeth stepped up to save him from the throng, intending to suggest that they head on home as it was getting late and she wanted to get the baby in bed soon.

She laughed as he was swept along by the tide of bodies, the one professor following behind still trying to make his points to no avail.

The group was headed across the street to a small café where many of the students gathered in between and after classes.

Elizabeth shouted that she would catch up with him. She wanted to pick up a few things for the baby while they were in town and was hoping John would show up soon.

He had said he would be late, but where was he?

She checked the baby, making sure she was content in her stroller. She was sound asleep.

Lawrence could still be seen as the group huddled into the cafe. Someone got the bright idea of locking the door behind them before the lone professor could enter.

He stood outside the window for a few moments, trying in vain to gather his dignity, before giving up and making his way down the street.

As he walked away, in the opposite direction of Elizabeth, he very violently stepped away from something in an alley. As he continued on, he grabbed his nose and waved his hand in the air to disperse some foul odor.

Elizabeth didn't see. She was on a mission for baby needs, thinking about just how lucky she had been to find the love of her life.

Both. Father and daughter.

Chapter Eighteen

That morning

The boy still loved to cause a commotion.

Morgana sat back and enjoyed the eruption of chaos around her. Outside Gilbert had been fished out of the fountain and given first aid, mouth-to-mouth resuscitation, and chest compressions to little avail.

The waiter was gone, just as Morgana had said.

Morgana picked at the rest of her breakfast, no longer really hungry. Of course, being immortal, eating was quite often one of those boring things you just had to do and get out of the way.

The cost of immortality was apparently losing interest in the taste of a fine wine or perfectly seared bit of fish or riding with the wind blowing through her hair.

Well, she assumed it would be things like that; the very idea of doing fun things had lost its appeal back in the Middle Ages.

Mordred, on the other hand, was still finding ways to amuse himself.

The apple didn't fall far from the tree apparently.

Chapter Nineteen

The Past

"Where is he?"

"He was just here a moment ago."

"Well, find him."

The door on the wardrobe was flung open and a beefy hand latched onto his arm. For a second, he thought of biting the hand to be free but reconsidered.

"I just wanted to see her," Lawrence said, pulled from his hiding spot.

"I'm afraid that might not be the best thing right now, young man," said the lady from the lady's society at the church, Mrs. Wicklewhite or something. She was a dour old thing who had been great friends with his late grandmother. Why, they had practically grown up together.

Young Lawrence stood his ground, his favorite book as his shield against the intruder while she stood there, arms crossed, a look so sour it made lemons look sweet. It was obvious the lady had her own opinions on the progeny of her great friend.

A number of such ladies had come around to help with things in their home with his mum taken ill.

He reckoned they meant well with their actions apart from the occasional "Tsk, would you look at?" and "Well, her mother was such a saint." Of course he heard those things.

"Now, come along, young man," Mrs. Wicklewhite said, one eyebrow arched so high he imagined it would almost touch her white helmet of hair. He figured he didn't like her much and suspected his gram probably never did either.

He stood his ground, having no intention of leaving his self-appointed post and allowing this white-haired maven to order him about. He was set on seeing his mother.

It was a standoff of epic forces, an immovable object against an impenetrable fortress. Or some such, he wasn't certain he had that last bit right, but oh well. He wasn't about to give up for her.

"I'll take young master Lawrence in hand, shall I?" said another of the ladies, a younger one, appearing in the doorway down the corridor. She extended her hand, smiling, but Lawrence still stood his ground.

Mrs. Wicklewhite snorted, "I could have told you this would happen."

The younger woman simply grinned and said, "Do you like lemon cakes? I just happened to have made a fresh batch and brought them."

The mention of anything lemon at that moment made him chuckle. And the icy standoff was broken as he took the lady's hand.

"Come. Bring your book and perhaps you might show me some things in it whilst we delve into a treasure trove of lemon cake, eh?"

She guided him out of the room past the dragon who said, "Don't go far, Cordelia."

"We'll just be in the garden, I think, Mrs. W.. Come along, my young knight, and join me in a repast of cakes of lemon and tales of the Table Round." She curtsied, making him laugh in spite of himself.

He answered with a low bow. "This way, my lady."

They made a brief stop in the kitchen and the one named Cordelia plucked a towel-covered tray from the kitchen table. The table was covered with various other dishes (casseroles and such, he figured). She also grabbed a tray with a teapot, two cups, some cream and sugar and beckoned him to open the door out into the small outside table in the garden.

Somehow, she managed to balance everything with nary a whoopsie and set it neatly upon the table.

Dropping his book onto one chair, he rushed around to get her chair for her.

"Thank you, my young knight."

"Welcome, miss," he said, seating himself, his book back on his lap.

"You may call me Cordelia, young master Lawrence," she said, pouring the tea. "Sugar?"

"Two, please."

"Cream?'"

"No, thank you...Cordelia."

"Lemon cake? I doubt you can refuse these!" she said, smiling as she whisked the towel from the plate to reveal cakes neatly stacked in concentric circles, a single muffin in the center.

"Presentation and symmetry. Very important when it comes to such things."

"Even in lemon cakes?"

"Oh, of course! You must pay attention to all details! Even in lemon cakes!"

She placed one on a plate with a fork, but he took it in his fingers and took a big bite off the end.

"Mmmmm."

"Good, eh?" she said, smiling as she watched him chew that mouthful, then sip his tea, careful not to drip any onto his book.

She gave it a few moments as she nibbled and sipped as well, then said, "I know this is a difficult time for you."

He nodded, looking back into the house. In the kitchen, one or two of the ladies were looking into the dishes on the table and others on the countertop. They were either judging each one or deciding which needed to be heated up or refrigerated. Probably being very judgy, he figured. They were trying very hard not to look at him, but he knew they were.

He just wanted to see his mother.

"In a bit, how's about we check in on your mum, shall we? See if she's up to eating a little something, eh?" Cordelia said, reaching over to wipe a crumb from the corner of his mouth. Her hand patted his cheek.

Her touch was gentle, but he could tell the skin on her hand was a bit rough. Calloused. He looked up to see her smiling at him and felt better. It was much like the tender smile his own mum gave him.

He liked this lady.

The others, though...

She motioned with her head toward the kitchen. "They aren't so bad, you know," she said as if reading his mind. "They try to do their best, the best they know how."

"Even that Mrs. Wicklewhite?"

She laughed, and it made him smile in spite of himself. "Well, she might be a special case."

"Very special," he said quietly.

"Mmm. Knowing who the good ones are will always be a good thing to know."

"Good ones like you?"

She smiled and looked just a little sad. "Even better than me. Lawrence, we choose how we face this old world every day when we wake up. For now, you must be brave."

"Like one of the Knights of the Round Table?"

"Exactly so."

He was quiet again for a bit, pinching a corner off his cake and popping it into his mouth.

"Will my mother be okay?"

"I can't tell the future. I know that she's very ill, so you must be extra brave in the days ahead. Can you do that?"

"I-I don't know if I can." He was trying very hard not to start crying.

'I know you can be strong. Like the knights."

"Did they ever cry?"

She paused and considered her reply before answering. "Even the strongest can know sorrow."

"Like King Arthur? Like, when Lancelot betrayed him?"

"Is that what your book says?"

He nodded and flipped the book open to a familiar page and showed it to her. Her brow furrowed, she read the page with interest.

"Yes, well, there is much more to the story than-" Something caught her attention suddenly.

"Lawrence, did you underline these letters here?"

"No, miss. I'm loathe to write in my books."

She flipped through the pages of the book to the first page with letters underlined and began reading them in order. She looked up suddenly.

"Lawrence, do you have a pencil and paper?"

"Yes, miss. There in the kitchen. Mother keeps it for notes and shopping lists. Shall I fetch it?"

"Yes, please."

The sister of The Sword lies within a sheath of wood spin three to the west then one fourth turn back then back again to north

She looked up slowly. Lawrence was just finishing off his cake.

"Lawrence, do you have any idea who might have written in your book?"

"My father perhaps."

"Do you know where he is?"

He was quiet for a moment. "He was killed in service."

"In the army?"

He shrugged, "I 'spose. That's what my gram told me. Then she died, too." Now, Cordelia could see the crack in the armor as his lip began to quiver.

He looked at her and said, "And now my mum...What's to happen to me if something happens to her?"

"We shall just have to work it out. I promise you. Alright?"

Lawrence thought about it a few moments then nodded.

He asked, "Do you have children?"

She smiled, "I hope to one day. But first, I must meet his or her father!"

"A shining knight?"

Laughing, she said, "I mean to find a good man to share my life, Lawrence. He needn't worry about saving me, just be a good husband and father."

"Besides, he would soon discover that I am no shrinking violet and need no saving. Unless it was the last lemon cake!" She tickled his ribs and made him giggle.

"Cordelia!"

Mrs. Wicklewhite stood at the door to the kitchen, hands on her hips.

"Yes, Mrs. W?"

"This is scarcely the time for frivolity! Now come, I have some things that need attending that require your care."

"Very well, Mrs. W." Cordelia said, standing and offering her hand to Lawrence, who took it with one hand, his prized book in his other. Shall we, sir knight?"

The pair marched into the kitchen past the stern matron.

Lawrence stopped and handed Cordelia the book then ran back outside to gather up the remains of their treat and walked them carefully back into the kitchen, putting them in the sink.

He turned to see Cordelia beaming at the manners the young gentleman showed. She handed his book back and they went to his bedroom, where she got him settled before leaving to see to a lengthy list of errands.

"I shall be back tomorrow and perhaps we can explore your book a bit more and we can read about an adventure or two with those brave knights, hm?"

"Yes, miss."

"More cakes tomorrow?"

"Yes, please. The lemon ones. They're my new favorite."

"Absolutely. Keep your spirits up and I'll see you on the morrow."

She kissed him on the forehead and gave him a hug before heading out. And she closed the gate behind her she felt as if she was being watched. Expecting it to be Lawrence, she turned to wave but was greeted instead by the stern scowl of Mrs. Wicklewhite from the front window before she closed the curtains.

When Cordelia finally returned the next day, a fresh batch of lemon cakes in a tin, she arrived to find the house oddly quiet.

Quiet and less furnished. Things were missing and there were boxes around with pictures and knick-knacks from the bookshelves.

Hearing noise down the hallway, she went to Lawrence's room and found one of the younger ladies of the society packing his things, no Lawrence in sight.

"Winifred, what's going on? What's happened? Where's Lawrence?"

"Oh, Cordelia, Mrs. Wicklewhite couldn't bear to see the poor lad so despondent, being in this dreadful situation as he is, and had him taken to her home to stay with her family."

"Wait, what? He was fine when I left."

"She was most insistent. She simply has a heart of gold, that one."

"Heart-of...Winifred, what about Amelia? Has the worst happened?" She started to head down the hallway, but the other woman caught her by the arm.

"She's gone, Cordelia."

"That quickly?"

"The doctor came soon after you left and they took her away."

"They who?"

'They. They! I only know what I was told and I was told to begin sorting and packing the boy's things. Just in case."

"What do you mean, just in case? Things were fine when I left."

Winifred was getting irritated at the continuing interruptions. "I simply don't know, Cordelia. You'll just have to ask Mrs. Wicklewhite."

"Oh, I intend to do just that."

Cordelia seethed and spotted a piece of paper on the floor. It was the sheet she had written the inscription on. She tucked it away and started to leave.

Winifred stopped her. "I hope those aren't more of those cakes of yours"

"They are."

"Mrs. W said to tell you they must have made the boy sick."

"Oh, she did, did she..."

A while later, she was on the steps of the Wicklewhite house.

Chapter Twenty

The recent past

They had agreed to have a quick honeymoon. In part, to save money for a house instead of the small apartment they now shared. It was close to Hampton where Lawrence could get back and start his second year as a professor.

Elizabeth ran the R&D department for a small company that did DNA studies and gene development.

Her inquisitive mind had followed that path primarily, although she had minor degrees in several disciplines including business and education. Some people told her she collected degrees like other women collected shoes. She couldn't help it if she had a thirst for knowledge and little patience for wasted time. She knew how lucky she was to find a man who wasn't threatened by her accomplishments.

With her position she could take all the time she wanted from the office since she always had her laptop with her and work was only a keystroke away.

"How's about a day trip to Chinatown in London?" Lawrence said.

She had never been to Chinatown and Lawrence had spent most of his youth very close to it. He knew all the great places to eat and the shops that really had the best finds for antiques and such.

A day spent walking around absorbing the culture had yielded some curios and souvenirs as well as a few books Elizabeth was pleased to add to her ever-growing library. Lawrence said, partially in jest, they might have to find a house just for their books.

"Well, then we will just need more bookshelves. How handy are you with a hammer and a saw?"

Lawrence laughed, "Not very. Although I do seem to remember a place somewhere near here that might fit the bill."

It was late afternoon and already the shadows had started to deepen. Their purchases tucked away in the trunk of the car, Elizabeth was ready to call it a day well spent.

"Really, the day is getting on, Lance. I thought we might have time to eat soon."

He looked at the woman he had married and caressed her cheek. Lance was her special nickname for him, especially when she was trying to get her way.

"Just one more place. It won't take long, I promise. We're close." As of yet, he hadn't found a pet name for her, but then they had the rest of their lives for that.

She sighed and smiled. "This is the last place, then food."

"Agreed!" and off they went, Lawrence taking the lead, sometimes almost pulling her along. Through shadowed streets they rushed, past other shops that might have something interesting, but Lawrence pressed on. He seemed as if on a mission, looking at the signs and sometimes down one street, then back the other way.

"Oh, look, what about that one?" she said, as they passed yet another.

"What else could you possibly hope to find?" he asked, eyes scanning the streets in hopes of catching a glimpse of something to remind him of the place he sought.

Elizabeth said, "I don't know, Lance, how about a samurai sword or something?"

"Exactly what we need: something sharp. And besides, that's Japanese, not Chinese," Lawrence replied.

"As if I didn't really know that…" she muttered, still being pulled along.

"What was that dear?" he asked, not really listening anyway.

"Nothing. Are we anywhere close to this place? My feet hurt after all this walking."

"Hm, I think…yes, through here." And down another narrow alleyway they went.

They had met in college both working with DNA research and fell in love at first sight. It took Lawrence a couple months to ask her out but from that first date on they were inseparable. She loved his dry humor and quick wit. He loved her right back in a way she felt he needed to be complete after many years without any real family.

This journey was testing her devotion though, she thought.

When they emerged from the alley, they found themselves on a street like many of the others, but apparently, Lawrence had found the one he had been searching for.

Outside, the little shop had all types of knick-knacks on display, of all kinds and sizes.

Porcelain figurines and delicate bird cages, some with birds inside singing to the unexpected company making their way into the store. The scents of exotic spices tinged the air. Paintings and framed scrolls adorned the walls.

As they ventured deeper into the shop, furniture was stacked to the ceiling. There were tables, chairs and cabinets of all shapes, styles and sizes.

But Lawrence's attention was on something in the rear of the shop, a tall ornate wardrobe in the far corner. Standing in front of it, he seemed mesmerized. In the center of each door was an inlaid circle with what looked like a crest of a dragon. His fingers traced over it without truly looking, as if it was already familiar.

Elizabeth watched him, fascinated, and said, "You know that won't fit in our apartment."

Lawrence answered as if in a fog, "I can't believe it. And this symbol..."

Elizabeth hadn't really looked at it that closely. All the oriental illustrations and trappings around them were starting to blend together in the cramped shop. And her stomach was rumbling.

Elizabeth "That doesn't really fit with all the other images. It seemed more medieval than Asian."

Lawrence continued "This can't be the same one..."

Elizabeth replied, "Could it have been here before? It was probably here the last time you were in this shop when you were younger. You must have been in this shop before."

Lawrence said, "Have I?"

He reached up and pushed on a decorative wood inlayed figure over the doors and the doors opened.

He tested both doors and opened them wide. "Well, what about that?" he said, as he gingerly felt the wood.

As he swung the doors closed again, a small Asian woman stood there, as if from nowhere, startling them both. Behind her, a man looked busy dusting off various things with a large feather duster. He had not been there before, either.

The woman looked at Elizabeth and then at Lawrence.

"We received that piece last month from a warehouse on the east side of London."

Lawrence looked at her and then at Elizabeth. "I grew up on the east side of London."

Elizabeth said "Lawrence, you said you grew up in homes all over London after your mom died when you were nine. Are you thinking that you've seen this very cabinet?"

"It's a wardrobe," said the old woman and Lawrence at the same time.

Lawrence continued, "There's definitely something familiar about it, as if I've seen it in a dream, but yes."

Elizabeth "Okay but it still won't fit in our apartment."

Lawrence continued to stand in front of the furniture looking at it. "Before my mom died, she had read me *Chronicles of Narnia: The Lion, the Witch and The Wardrobe*. It was the last book we read together. The night we finished the book I had a dream, and, in my dream, I was fighting something and what I needed to beat it was hidden in this wardrobe."

"I believe it was mine."

"It may have been." said the old lady.

The man tried in vain to look over her shoulder without being obvious but she gently nudged him with her elbow and he went back to pretending to be preoccupied with his dusting.

Lawrence opened the cabinet again and looked around inside. He stepped in, closing the door behind him.

Elizabeth opened the door to the wardrobe. He sat inside, smiling, and getting teary-eyed. The last time he had been inside, his mother was dying down the hall and he was hiding from that white-haired Mrs. Wicklewhite.

Tears ran down her own face at the sight of him, imaging the boy he would have been, about to face the greatest loss of his life.

He stepped out, kissed her gently and wiped her tears away as she did the same to him.

Then he turned back to the wardrobe and closed the door. He fingered the carved images of the dragons, following the curves of the figures and the edges of the circles. He pushed on one of the dragon figures and it opened to reveal a small piece of paper. He pulled the paper out.

She took it from his trembling fingers.

It read:

The sister of The Sword lies within a sheath of wood spin three to the west then one fourth turn back then back again to north.

"What does it mean?" she asked.

Carefully, he moved the right inlaid circle and pushed on it. It seemed to give just a little.

click

Then he turned the whole thing anti-clockwise three times until the dragon was again upright.

click

Then a quarter-turn clockwise.

CLICK

And back to its regular position.

Inside the cabinet there came a definite click and Lawrence opened the door to reveal an open panel on the inside of the door.

There was something inside.

Lawrence reached in as Elizabeth and the shopkeepers watched, mesmerized.

Inside was a sword still in its scabbard.

Elizabeth, her mouth wide open, looked from Lawrence to the old Asian woman and man then back to Lawrence.

The sword was over three feet long. Tattered rags had been stuffed into the recess to keep it from rattling around, some of them falling out onto the floor as Lawrence undid small leather straps that held it in place.

Taking it out of its hiding place, the rest of the rags fell onto the floor of the shop, kicking up dust from some previous age. The old man swatted at it with his duster as he sneezed.

The pommel at the end of the hilt bore the same ornate dragon symbol as on the door of the wardrobe.

"What the…" Elizabeth started to reach forward but the old man stopped her, his hand out.

"That will be one hundred and fifty pounds for the sword."

Lawrence gave the man a look, "What?"

"One hundred and fifty pounds." The old Asian man said and tried to grab the sword from Lawrence's hand.

Startled, Lawrence looked at Elizabeth. Elizabeth replied, "You're not hanging that thing on my walls." And smiled.

Elizabeth looked at the woman. "I'll give you 50 pounds."

"No, one hundred and fifty," he said again.

He tried to grab it again but a hand from behind him pulled him back.

The man angrily whirled around to face the woman. She gave him a withering stare and said nothing. The man meekly nodded and went back to dusting.

Elizabeth said to the woman, "Look, I have seventy-five pounds and not a pound more."

The old woman looked at Lawrence. "No need." Behind her, the man made a noise in spite of himself. "It belongs to him. Obviously. He must take the wardrobe and sword."

Elizabeth looked up from the woman at Lawrence, who hadn't taken his eyes off the sword. Elizabeth touched his shoulder and he jumped. As if he had been in a trance.

"How did I figure out the combination to open that panel?"

Elizabeth leaned in and whispered "Lawrence, believe me, I've seen some weird stuff running around with my Uncle John. Come on, let's go home and study this thing."

"What about the wardrobe?"

"It will be safe here for now," the woman said. She closed the door to the cabinet, and it clicked and locked itself. She looked at Elizabeth.

"For safekeeping. I will hold it until you can arrange to retrieve it. I promise no one will touch it until then. Except perhaps to dust it". She gave the man a brief look. He suddenly decided he needed to dust as far from her as he could.

"Well, I can't just take a sword out on the street, even sheathed. He started trying to wrap the rags around it to hide what it was.

"I believe it will fit in that guitar case behind you. Just don't answer if someone asks you to play, hm?"

The dusting man threw his hands up in exasperation at her sudden penchant for giving the whole store away.

The sword secured, Lawrence and Elizabeth left the shop after giving the woman their information so they could arrange for the wardrobe later.

As they left, Elizabeth said, "Well, now we may have to get a house just to have somewhere to put that thing."

The woman watched them until they were out of sight and out of earshot, then made a call. The man started to come closer but a stern look from her stopped him cold and he went the other way. With haste.

The phone rang a few times on the other end before someone picked up.

The woman said, "The boy found his tooth."

"Thank you."

Chapter Twenty-One

Later that morning

In Brixton, there sat an old dusty warehouse where nothing of any value was stored, a forgotten place hidden away amongst other old warehouses and abandoned shops.

Inside the old warehouse, one would not expect to find much but shadows and things with tarpaulin coverings gathering more dust.

A typical old warehouse one might suppose, but for one exception here, though. The shadows moved. Well, less like shadows and more like bundles of moving dank and dark rags. If one could catch the aroma given off, one might very well find him or herself purging any last meals eaten. And then some.

Evil prevailed here. More than the stench. Well, perhaps it intensified the smell, making it reek even worse. It was difficult to say since few would even see past the ragged and see little more than a mounting homeless population.

In the far rear was a small office, barren of any sense of style but cluttered with stacks of ledgers, lunch wrappers, and notebooks. On the walls faded maps sprouted colored pins, most of them in the British Isles, some in the American colonies, others sprinkled around the world.

One shelf, barely hanging on, sported several miniature ships inside crusty old glass milk bottles.

Inside the office, a single light glowed, barely illuminating a man at a large old desk fiercely intent on the current task at hand.

"Gently. Gently…"

Fingers thick as sausages carefully manipulated slender tongs holding the mast of a ship in place.

"Almost…"

A sudden noise at the door startled him, causing the tongs to snap the mast, ruining it.

"Bugger!"

He dropped the bottle onto the desk and threw the tongs down then whipped around to confront the vile wretch who had interrupted him.

"What have I told you, you little-??"

Standing at the doorway was a mountain of a man dressed in a three-piece suit. The last time Moog had seen him, ten years previous, he had been much more imposing, more dangerous.

The battle over some little snot in the Dragon's bloodline had decimated him for a time and it had taken years to regain his full strength.

Well, almost.

He was a formidable man and Moog would not, even on his best day, have challenged him.

Mordred.

"Go on, Moog, finish that sentence. I dare you!" he challenged.

For one so big himself, although not in any sort of muscular way, Moog quickly fell from the chair onto his knees.

"Apologies, Master! I thought it was one of those Hounds outside pestering me again."

A chorus of hisses from without followed, having been blamed needlessly. Moog clambered to his feet and roared out into the darkness past his master.

"Shut your gobs, you useless piles of excrement!" He braced himself and turned back to the imposing man now looking over his milk bottle handiwork.

"Again, my apologies, Master. With fewer targets lately, they've been a bit restless."

"They're Hounds, Moog. What do you hope to have them sniff out in this rat trap? Each other? Better to sniff through rubbish bins. I don't care if they have to wander the streets of every town and every burg from here to Australia."

The Master ventured ominously close to the shelves of milk bottle ships, his breath fogging each one as he peered inside.

Moog held his breath and his tongue.

Mordred cast a glance at Moog and raised an eyebrow. Moog instantly felt embarrassed, as if he were a schoolboy found cheating by the schoolmaster.

"Oh, those? A hobby. They help me think."

"They clearly aren't working." He picked up the work-in-progress from the desk and looked inside.

Moog moved closer, his hands suspended in front of him as if he might have to catch the thing. Then whipped them behind his back when Mordred gave him a look.

"I know this ship." the Master said.

"Um, yes, you should, milord. It's The Morgana. You should know it well. That was the voyage you took to reap the spawn of that fool Percival."

"Which ended in disaster!" the Master said, noting the hole in the side of the ship.

"Through no fault of your own, milord. Who knew the bloodline would prove too stubborn to be deleted?"

"Mm."

Caught up in the excitement of explaining his recreation, Moog ventured closer to point out "And if you look closer, you'll see where the bodies of his retinue are strung up on the aft mast flying in the breeze like flags to your vengeance."

"And still the cur escaped."

"Well, yes. Through no fault of yours…"

"And helped to establish contact with those in the New World who have ever since been even greater thorns in my side."

"And your mother's, yes."

Mordred whipped around with a look even Moog feared to catch a glimpse of.

"That witch!"

"Your mother?"

"Of course, my mother, you toad. Who else has me at their beck and call?"

"But she's your mother."

"Feh."

"Ummm,"

"Summon those piles of fetid rags out there and find me some knights' whelps to slay before she uses my own body against me.

"Master?"

"Nothing. An old wound she keeps reopening when she's in the mood."

"There are other forces out there at work, helping them. Find them as well."

"Yes, Master. Look alive, you wretches! You know what I mean…"

"May I have my bottle back?"

Chapter Twenty-Two

The shop was quiet now, but Moog's hands still trembled slightly. It always took him some time to gather his wits after an encounter with his master. And an unexpected one at that.

The ship in the bottle was a disaster. Maybe moving on to a different project would settle his nerves.

Moog put the final touches on a new project, a diorama of the attack on the tobacco shop from ten years previous.

He had run out of ship ideas. Or perhaps out of milk bottles. Not that it mattered.

Chapter Twenty-Three

The rain began to come down harder so Elizabeth decided it might be time to cut her shopping short and return to the lecture hall and Lawrence.

There was still no more sign of her Uncle John, so she rang him up to make sure nothing serious was the matter.

When he told her what had happened and to be alert, her blood ran cold. The ragged figure in the auditorium…

Something in her voice caused him to question whether something was happening there as well. They could have brunch sometime soon. She tried to reassure him that nothing was wrong so he should simply turn around and go home, but he was having none of it.

Even so, she chose not to alarm him about the strange figure in the back corner of the lecture hall. She was afraid he would only speed up faster and have another accident.

Finally, she told him to head to their house and they would discuss it.

Leaving the New and Used Babies Are Here store she loved to visit when they were in town, she decided to find Lawrence. It was high time they headed home.

As she rounded the corner to make her way back to the cafe, she could swear she saw the same dark figure from the lecture hall across the street from the café. It was focused intently on the small group of figures gathered around a table in the middle of the café's window.

She crossed the street to the side of the café away from the figure. The dark thing quickly and almost animalistically turned its head toward her. The way it shook its head reminded her of a dog sniffing the air as it leaned toward her. The figure started to move toward her so she stopped under the cover of a small storefront's canopy on the sidewalk just a few doors down from the café. She reached in the bundle of blankets and touched a small object that sat next to her baby's side.

The figure stopped and looked around and around as if she had just vanished.

Confused and frustrated at having lost her somehow the figure stepped back on the sidewalk and headed away in the opposite direction.

Holding her breath when she reached into the blankets, she finally exhaled. Not trusting the figure would not return she pushed the stroller bent over keeping in contact with the charm.

As she entered the café Lawrence met her gaze and knew something was amiss. He quickly excused himself from the group and met Elizabeth just a few steps into the shop.

"What's wrong?" Lawrence said as Elizabeth stood up from the stroller.

"Uncle John is going to meet us at home. We need to leave now," was her reply.

As they headed toward their car, Lawrence took charge of the stroller while Elizabeth explained seeing the figure earlier in the lecture hall and then just before she joined him in the cafe.

And, that something wasn't right.

"I'm telling you, Lawrence, when I reached in and touched the charm he couldn't see me," Elizabeth explained.

They reached their car in the parking space set aside for faculty just as it began to sprinkle again.

While Lawrence buckled Angela into her seat Elizabeth looked around, scouring the shadows of the buildings and shrubbery.

Angela awoke just long enough to try to touch his face. He nibbled her little fingers and kissed them as she yawned and fell asleep again once she was snug.

He hurried to open Elizabeth's door for her as the sky seemed to empty up with a deluge. He started the engine and turned the heater on to help dry them out.

They started the long drive to the outer edges of western Croydon just as the rain began again.

"In the short time that we've been married you've told me about a few of the wild adventures that you and your Uncle John had gone on. Collecting trinkets…"

Elizabeth interrupted, "Charms and relics."

Lawrence corrected himself "All right, as you say, charms and relics. You've never told me what your Uncle did with them and why he would endanger himself and you to find them."

"I've told you. My grandfather was hurt, and he needed them to recover."

"Yes, but how was he injured and how would the trink- uh, charms help him recover?"

"You know this is complicated. It's like when we found the sword in the old China shop months ago. You still don't have a clue how you knew to open the hidden department. But you did. There's more than just trinkets and charms. There's…"

She hesitated and then continued. "There are creatures… vile, evil creatures that want these charms and more and want to see the bloodlines of the round table knights eradicated."

"Elizabeth, you're sounding like the vice chancellor now. Next, you're going to tell me that these creatures have magical powers and can follow smell or scent."

"No, not exactly. It's our blood," Elizabeth replied.

Lawrence had just turned down a side road as a shortcut home. The road was dark with an upper ridge on the right with a silhouette of trees. The rain was starting to let up some.

Lawrence turned to Elizabeth. "What exactly do you mean by blood?"

"And what do you mean by our blood?"

Chapter Twenty-Four

The rain had picked up since leaving the little café and it was making the roads even harder to maneuver. Lawrence was trying to concentrate on driving after asking Elizabeth about the blood thing when he heard her say "Are you listening to me?"

"Of course, I am... What?" he replied.

"The DNA research has not only shown us the bloodlines, but it also has discovered a mutated gene. We're calling it a magi gene."

"By we you mean you and your famous grandfather I've never met, and magi means "magic", correct?" Lawrence said as things were getting a little tense. The driving was becoming harder, and they were still only halfway home.

He continued "How many times have you found this magi gene?"

She replied "Twice…well, actually three times."

Lawrence looked at her "Seriously, three times?"

"Yes, two connected samples and a single one from another bloodline. The single was the stronger of the two."

"What bloodlines!?" About then a lightning bolt struck right near the side of the car. Lawrence overcorrected but straightened the car back onto the road.

"Sure glad no one was coming toward us."

"You know we haven't had a car pass us in a few miles."

Boom.

Another loud clap of thunder, then another lightning strike, this time to the left of the car.

Lawrence "What the-?"

"It's as if the lightning is trying to strike us!" Elizabeth shouted.

"Oh, blueberries."

Chapter Twenty-Five

Fourteen Months Earlier...

The streak of lightning was a bit too close for comfort, so he picked up his pace. He was on a mission!

It was a stormy little day, but Lawrence had things that needed doing as he made his way down the rainy street. His umbrella was next to useless as the wind whipped around a bit, but he was determined to see his errand through.

He entered a small bakery just off campus where he hoped to get something special for Elizabeth.

Just the day before, she had surprised him with the announcement that they were going to be parents.

He wasn't certain that they were ready, but he loved his wife and decided to get her something special for dessert tonight.

Perhaps it was him that wasn't ready. The thought had occurred to him and nagged at him. With his childhood being the way it was, how could he not think about it?

If only his mother had lived. Or his father. Or if only…

If only, if only, if only…

If only it would stop raining, he thought as a car passed and hit a puddle, splashing him.

Earlier that morning he had contacted the bakery and asked if they could make a Christmas Cake. Admittedly, they were a little surprised at the request as Christmas was still months away and that it wasn't the easiest of baked goods to make in such a short period of time.

After explaining what a special occasion it was the baker on the other end of the phone line said she would do her very best and have one for him before closing time that day.

Lawrence had left the college late and hoped that the bakery was still open. He was in a hurry to leave and, of course, that was when every little thing that could delay him tried to do just that. But he was determined, no matter what.

And wonder of wonders, even though it was a little past closing, the door was open. Inside, the baker met him at the counter with a box decorated with a large pink ribbon and bow in honor of the occasion.

"Pink?" he asked, an eyebrow raised.

"I just had a hunch," the baker, whose apron had an embroidered Cecilia in the corner, smiled. "And just in case, there's a blue one underneath the cake box on the off-chance I'm wrong. Promise you'll let me know!"

"I promise," he said with a nod and a bow.

"I must confess, my average so far is in the high-80s percentile."

"Well, I'm not sure if I've had enough time to even process the thought of being a father just yet, but girl or boy, this child will have a beautiful mother."

She had used more blueberries than candied fruit in the Christmas cake than usual, but she hoped his wife would enjoy the surprise.

"I must tell you that baking this today for you brought back many wonderful memories of my father and working in his bakery when I was a little girl," Cecilia said, smiling.

"You come from a family of bakers, I take it?" replied Lawrence.

"Oh yes, my father had a bakery in Brixton."

Lawrence stopped, surprised.

"It wouldn't have been near Elm Street, by any chance?"

"Why, yes, did you know it?"

"My wife grew up in Brixton until her uncle passed. He owned a tobacconist on Elm Street."

It was Cecilia's turn to be surprised.

"Do you mean George's and Anne's place?"

"That's the one." replied Lawrence.

"Oh my! I remember Mr. Leo Degrance had taken in his niece before I moved away to college. So, Elizabeth is your wife? What a small world!" the baker exclaimed.

Lawrence smiled at the coincidence. "Yes, it is."

"Please bring her sometime! I would love to meet her and talk about our old neighborhood."

"I shall do just that." Lawrence replied and started for the door.

Leaving the baker waving through the window as she closed up her shop for the day, Lawrence felt the incredible sense of loss in his wife's life on that street which ended with her and her aunt Anne almost being killed by a maniac with a sword. He had heard the story a few times, mostly from her Uncle John.

Chapter Twenty-Six

Now...

BOOOM!!

The lightning hit so close he felt the car lurch. Or was it him?

"Blueberries," Lawrence said to no one in particular as he gripped the wheel tighter.

Elizabeth jerked her head toward him and asked, "What?"

"What? Oh. Blueberries are your favorite, aren't they?"

"Yes, but what brought that up?"

"I was just thinking about the Christmas Cake that I brought home the day after you told me about being parents. And how Cecilia had used more blueberries than candied fruit."

"It was storming that day, but nothing like this."

Elizabeth leaned over, kissed him on the cheek and said, "You are simply adorable. Yes, blueberries are my favorite. And there was a pink ribbon and bow on the box. Remind me, who is supposed to be related to a famous detective in this family?"

Lawrence replied, "Well, I married her, so she must be rubbing off on me."

A lightning bolt flashed across the road in front of them, hitting a tree off to the side. With a groan, it fell and blocked the road. Lawrence swerved to miss it, but the car started to slide on the wet roadway.

Lawrence struggled to regain control, but the car and wet pavement were having none of it. He tried pumping the brake and steering into the curve, everything, and anything he could ever think to avoid a crash.

He almost had it under control he thought when the front tire caught the edge of the road. The move startled him and caused him to overcorrect, and the car was totally out of control at that point.

Beside him, Elizabeth braced herself and instinctively reached back for Angela.

The car rolled up the embankment, threatening to flip over but Lawrence cut the wheel back toward the side and hit the ditch, launching the vehicle back onto the pavement with a violent jolt, causing the airbags to deploy.

Mashing the brake with all he could muster, Lawrence fought the car going into a spin and lost that battle. Finally, it stopped just before colliding with the fallen tree.

Barely aware, he was able to pull his pen from his jacket pocket and deflated his airbag. Then Elizabeth's.

She said, "Is it over?"

Then came the screams.

Chapter Twenty-Seven

William paced the hallway from the foyer to the kitchen. Earlier his plan had been to enjoy a bit of butter on bread, laced with honey from his beehives.

Then this ordeal had begun and the news from Watson wasn't good at all.

Finally, after the umpteenth time (he knew the number exactly but for the sake of hyperbole he generalized how many) he changed course to one of his private studies. He had several, each with its own focus.

This one sat behind an oaken door. Inside was a round table, probably not as large as the one at fabled Camelot.

Bookshelves, filled with tomes and novels of the legend of Arthur and his knights, lined the wall to the left.

On the opposite wall were clippings, pictures, and notes with colored bits of string leading from one thumbtack to another.

On the wall facing the door was a large map of the world. Notes were scribbled on bits of paper and tacked on, some with several layers as new information was discovered or sorted out, flags of different colors and sizes on pins dotted the continents.

It was this map he went to.

Yes, the news from Watson was bad, bad enough to prompt Holmes to finally call-in reserves. All of them he could. The time he had taken to dissect the situation was valuable time lost.

He found a pin tacked into England nearest the university where Lawrence was teaching. Spotting other places of importance, he made mental notes and rushed back to the nearest phone in the kitchen.

Curse his penchant for not having one in the study but he did not like to be disturbed when he was in thought.

But now...

Another man might have panicked but nonesuch was the man standing in his kitchen punching the buttons on a phone on the wall.

On the other end of the line, someone answered.

William didn't wait for courtesies and launched into a brief explanation.

"Call in the reserves! As many as you can reach and tell them the Beast is out and about. They'll know what that means. The destination is Snowflake. Send them now!"

He slammed the receiver back onto the cradle and wondered if there was another call he needed to make. Or two. There were powerful forces at work on both sides of the coin and his granddaughter and her family were in danger.

He looked out his kitchen windows at his new beehives. Life was so much simpler only hours before. Well, not really, no. For one such as himself, there were constant mysteries and riddles of the world being worked out in his magnificent mind.

Oh, for a good old-fashioned crime to solve right now.

Well, not right now obviously...

"Damn it, John, you old fool, he said, wishing Watson could hear him. "You really should have taken my man with you."

"And a bazooka."

He picked up the receiver and started dialing again.

Would they get there in time?

Chapter Twenty-Eight

Camelot The Past...

"What is it?"

"I call it a Merlin's Gate."

"I see no gate."

"Oh, Lancelot, really. I can't believe you were raised by the Lady of the Lake and never learned to take things as you see them."

One last mission, Merlin had said. Go collect dirt needed for his very secret project and return quickly.

And he had.

Upon returning to Camelot, the wizard welcomed him into his tower but instead of going up, they went down, and down, down into the hill behind the tower, coming at last into Merlin's workshop.

He was ushered through a stout wooden door adorned with many strange symbols into a large hall where shelves were stuffed with scrolls and bottles and cloth bags, much like the ones he had collected for the mage. He had the feeling of something watching but could find no set of glowing eyes peering out anywhere.

Possibly just his imagination.

On a lower level visible from the upper was a large round table with a patchwork of different-colored bits of dirt forming a…

Map?

"So, where is the gate, Merlin?"

Merlin sighed. Loudly.

Lancelot threw his arms up, "I see no gate. Only bits of dirt on a table."

Merlin's face lit up. "There, you, see? The bits of dirt! Each a sample of somewhere in the kingdom!"

"So, it is a map?"

"Exactly!"

"Where's the gate then?"

"You are looking at it."

"I'm confused, Merlin."

"Really? How can you tell any difference from any other day?"

"Well, then, what are those bits that almost look cloudy? There's nothing there?"

"Ah, I'm glad you asked!" the older face said, taking the bags of dirt Lancelot had brought him. He took a pinch from one, recited some odd words and ran the dirt between his fingers to fall below. As the dirt fell, it swirled in the air and wafted over the map to finally land in one of the fuzzy areas Lancelot had indicated.

Then he did another. And another. A pinch from each bag and soon much of that area of the map was filled in as well.

Lancelot watched, fascinated, and he started to understand.

"The dirt on the map is linked to the actual place."

Merlin burst into laughter, not a usual occurrence. And somehow, unsettling.

"Now he sees."

"And you can go there somehow."

"You are your mother's son, after all. Now, it's time for you to go. I have more work to do."

Lancelot nodded, his mind a little overwhelmed at the way of the world, seen and unseen. He thanked the wizard for finally sharing this with him and made to leave. Merlin stopped him before he left.

"Be mindful, Lancelot. There is another mother and son pairing that would sway the balance of things in Camelot for the worst. Evil things are afoot in the land and that woman is up to no good."

"You should tell Arthur."

"I have, several times, but he refuses to believe it of his own sister. Before you go, look at the map. That last dark patch will play a key role in things ahead."

"That is the land of Morgana's father. And the dirt you brought can open a gate close to it."

"But, why?"

"Beware, Lancelot. Beware."

Chapter Twenty-Nine

From outside the car, there was a screaming noise ringing in Lawrence's ears. He shut his eyes tight against the piercing sound to little avail.

Slowly, it dulled, and he could open his eyes and look around.

He realized the sound was in fact a high-pitched hissing coming from the engine somewhere under the hood.

His face hurt from the air bag. His neck hurt from the jolt. He shook his head to try clearing it and looked at Elizabeth, who had a small cut above her right eye which was bleeding.

"Liz?" he asked, gently reaching for her face, realizing as he did his hand was trembling.

She looked at him, unsteady herself. "I'm fine, I think."

"What about-?" They both quickly turned to see the baby sitting in her safety seat smiling and waving her hands, jingle ball tinkling just out of reach.

"A charmed life. Literally."

They laughed nervously at having evaded a wreck. Lawrence touched her cheek, careful not to brush anywhere near her cut.

He handed her his kerchief to hold on it to staunch the bleeding and said, "I love you."

Elizabeth replied "I lo-...

Boom.

Elizabeth screamed as something landed on the roof of the car.

Lawrence tried to start the car but the engine wouldn't turn over. The hissing came from under the crushed hood, steam rising from beneath it.

"It won't start."

A blinding light from an approaching car hit them directly in the face. The rain has picked up again. The car stopped about fifty meters from them, leaving their lights directly facing the couple.

Some kind of hand with long fingers and nails reached down and scratched across the front windshield as the creature leapt from the top of the car and landed about ten feet in front of the approaching car, blocking some of the light. The creature was slightly bent over and looked to be wearing a ragged coat.

Lawrence "What is that?"

"A bloodhound." Elizabeth replied without hesitation.

"That's like no dog I've ever seen!"

The creature turned its head and looked directly at them. Through the lights and rain Elizabeth could make out that the creature seemed to have a scar down its face where its right eye should have been.

Elizabeth "Oh, that's just bloody wonderful."

Chapter Thirty

Eight years earlier.

Elizabeth had begged her Uncle John to take her just once on a simple errand for her Great Grandfather.

Their mission that day was to pick up a small carved wooden bowl that John explained would help her great-grandfather heal from the injuries he had acquired during her rescue from the tobacco shop attack.

She had always felt guilty he was hurt helping her and her aunt Anne escape the monster, but John would repeat in that uncle-y way of his that one simply does what one can to protect family.

John Watson himself had no family still living. He had only his truest friend, with whom he had been on many adventures through the years and Elizabeth, his niece not by blood but by...well, that was just how it was.

Both of which he would do anything to protect.

They had left her aunt Anne on the farm with some helper tending fall crops. Her aunt still missed her late husband, their old home and the smoke shop but the farm gave her many things to do, distractions to ease her mind in such things. That included growing their own food and tending the few animals they kept, animals that had become more like pets than mere livestock.

Even so, Anne worried whenever Elizabeth ventured out into the wide world. Life had been so cruel to her already, robbing her of her parents at an early age, her uncle and the only homes she had known. Until now. The world was full of bad things, she knew. Some of them meant for her niece, she expected, but resolved not to be anxious about what might come or what might not. Life was too, too short for not living.

That was little comfort as she watched them drive away on their errand.

John and Elizabeth had driven through the night arriving at last at the edge of a small town. The sun was just starting to break above the massive hills that sat behind the town.

John pulled down a street that was mostly dirt and old stones. The car lurched left and right as he drove around obstacles and garbage cans littering the street.

There didn't appear to be much of anyone on the street itself, or in the whole town for that matter, although Elizabeth had the distinct feeling of being watched from curtained windows and darkened doorways.

John pulled around a corner onto a street of what looked like a row of rarely used shops. One had a faded green awning on an old building. A light shone from the inside. As he stopped the car nearby, the front window of the store exploded outward.

John cursed, "Not again. I'm not about to lose another one. My, dear, could you reach into the back seat and hand me my medical bag?"

"Oof, this is heavier than I expected," she said, pulling the bag to the front and handing it to him.

He reached in and pulled out a largish purple gem and handed it to Elizabeth, folding her fingers over it.

"Your snowflake charm will keep anything from seeing you but this will protect you. If something should happen to me you need to make it to the next town east of here, go down this street there and follow it out. Go to the postal service and ask for Mr. Burton. Tell him who you are, and he'll make sure you make it home to the farm."

"Uncle, nothing is going to happen." Elizabeth replied.

"Of course not, my dear, but you must always have a plan just in case."

"I love you, my dear."

She reached up and pulled the sleeve of his jacket and she gave him a kiss on his cheek and whiskers. "I'm never letting anything happen to my family again, Uncle."

He smiled and exited the car heading to the back of the shop into the dark. He had been gone awhile when she heard another loud boom and the back door exploded. She had been as patient as possible and decided that her Uncle may need some help. She exited the car and headed around the front of the store.

She saw a figure hanging out the front window that had exploded when they arrived. She first feared that it was her Uncle and quickly realized that it was a woman.

She looked into the store and saw two figures circling her Uncle. He was clutching a small object she couldn't quite make out and in his other hand he was holding something that was glowing and keeping the figures away. Elizabeth had enough and stepped into the store. John waved her away. "Elizabeth, get out of here."

The figures turned toward her and then back toward John then back toward her but not directly. As if they couldn't see her. The figures were some kind of creatures from her nightmares. They were bent over wearing rags as clothes with long arms and hands with nasty nails. Their heads had a canine look to them with a jutted jaw, but it was the eyes, light blue and swirls of green, that caused Elizabeth to hold the stone firmly in front of her as it began to glow. The creature closest to her turned and its eyes widened as if she just magically appeared.

The stone glowed brighter as it blasted the creature, burning the right side of its' face. It fell to the ground clutching its wound.

The other creature looked confused, so John took advantage of the opportunity and blasted the second creature, just barely hitting its left arm but causing the creature to retreat.

Elizabeth ran to her Uncle. "Are you hurt?" she asked, looking for any signs of injury.

"The second creature got a drop on me and surprised me," he replied.

"Next time we go together." Elizabeth practically pulled her Uncle out of the shop, then looked back at the creature holding its face. It looked at her with hate and disgust with the only eye it had left. She looked at the wretched thing and wondered if she should just finish it off.

Elizabeth bent down and picked up a jagged stick of lumber laying on the floor from the explosions.

She started walking toward the burnt-faced creature, careful to not let her guard down.

"Elizabeth, we don't kill. Not even these things."

'The stick is for protection. It was one of them that tried to kill me and Auntie."

"No, girl, it was something much worse than this creature. Leave it before more things or something much worse come."

She stood over the thing holding its face and prodded the creature with the stick.

"Hey," she said.

It looked up with a look of hatred and fear.

"You leave my family alone. Do you understand?"

The thing looked to the left and right but not at her.

She poked it again. "DO. YOU. UNDERSTAND?"

At last, it sighed, bowed its head, and slowly closed its eye.

She stepped back. "Good. Now, go. Before I change my mind!

Chapter Thirty-One

Now...

The rain had slowed down.

The creature stared long and hard directly at Elizabeth. The snowflake charm was tucked into the baby's seat. This thing could see her! Then it began to move toward the other car as the door opened.

A huge figure emerged from the car. Even fifty meters away they could tell that it was big. Elizabeth knew instantly it was him.

As a child she had called the evil creature the Dark Knight.

The thing had attacked her and her aunt and hurt her great-grandfather and haunted her dreams for years. Now he was back to finish what he wanted to do years ago: kill her and her family.

Lawrence looked at Elizabeth. "Your Uncle isn't that far behind us. I want you to take Angela, protect yourselves with the snowflake charm and head back down the road."

Elizabeth yelled back, "No! We all can use the charm and escape!"

Lawrence "We have no clue how many people that tiny thing can hide but we do know it worked for both of you earlier if you're close to it. This thing knows someone was driving this car so we can't all just disappear."

Elizabeth turned away from him. "I can't lose you... I won't..."

Lawrence interrupted her, "Elizabeth, you have to protect our baby at all costs."

Elizabeth turned back to him, a tear running down the side of her face mixing with the drops of rain.

It wasn't a look of sadness, though. He knew that look. No, she was getting angry, angrier than when she saw some injustice go unpunished. Angry that she had been put in the position of having to choose between staying and running away... Angry, because she knew Lawrence didn't stand a chance against this creature... Angry, because she knew she didn't have a choice but to protect Angela even if it meant deserting her husband.

"How do you expect to slow this thing down?" Elizabeth said in a voice that may have sounded more condescending than she intended.

Lawrence replied with a slight smile. "You aren't the only one that has been carrying around a charm."

Elizabeth looked at him with surprise. "What are you talking about?"

Lawrence looked at her now very seriously. "You are my heart and my soul…"

Elizabeth joined him "I will love you here and beyond forever and forever." It was part of their wedding vows they had written together.

Lawrence looked back and said, "Little Angel, protect your mum, she's going to need a lot of loving."

He opened the car door and tried to make out what was past the headlights. All he could really see was a big, shadowed figure moving along with two smaller figures. One was bent down almost like a large dog, the other was the creature that had landed on their car.

He moved around to the back of the car and opened the hatch. Elizabeth looked hard at him as she moved into the back seat next to Angela.

The large creature bellowed in response to her moving the snowflake closer to her.

Elizabeth said, "It knows I'm here."

Lawrence replied, "Well, I have something that will distract it!" and he pulled out the long sword that he had found in the cabinet from his childhood.

"I have my own charm... if it's what you think it is then I'm betting it has a little of its own magic. I've been taking lessons on campus with the fencing team."

And with that he smiled grimly as he took off his jacket. Then he steeled himself and advanced on the creatures.

She shouted after him, "Lawrence!"

He looked back at her and said, "I love you both." and started to advance on their attackers.

Chapter Thirty-Two

Elizabeth had called John when they took the shortcut home, so he had decided to stay on their trail in case something happened on the side of the road.

There was something in her voice that made John drive faster even though she had expressed that he should take his time.

He knew he should, especially after his last accident that had totaled one of his friends' cars. He still didn't believe it was his fault that the car jumped off the road and hit a guardrail. Something must have broken in the front end of the car.

He also knew driving wasn't one of his strengths. He had damaged more than one vehicle over the years and frequently stated he preferred a horse and buggy, to which his friend William would state that if he depended on a horse and buggy then most likely the horse would die.

At the moment he was glad for all the modern conveniences of a car. Windshield wipers in particular.

The rain was pouring down, making it harder to see the road.

Onward he went, trying to keep his speed in mind as the skies opened up.

Chapter Thirty-Three

Lawrence had believed the fact that Elizabeth and her Aunt had been attacked by something back in her uncle's tobacco shop but he didn't believe it was a monster as much as a little girl's perspective of the attack.

It wasn't until the moment he stepped forward to face the things attacking his family the word flashed through his mind.

Monsters.

He believed.

Steeling himself for whatever might come, he glanced back at the car that for now was shielding the true purpose of his life: his family. Something that he never had growing up and had wondered if he could ever have after losing his mother.

Then he met Elizabeth with her crazy stories and the life she had running around with her Uncle John. Lawrence had fallen in love with her the first time they had met. And each day after.

So, he had done it. Achieved the best things his life could ever have offered: a wife and a daughter And he was willing to do whatever it took to protect them from harm.

Lawrence steadied himself, feeling the weight of the sword. What had once seemed so heavy and awkward felt lighter and more a part of him after so many afternoon hours sparring with the members of the fencing club.

At the time, it sounded so silly to give in to the notion of wielding a sword. So silly he had kept it from Elizabeth. Not to hide it but surprise her one day with his prowess and impress her. Silly indeed since he knew she was already impressed with him.

It was something he needed for himself really. He thought of his book about the knights of the Round Table, of trying to be brave for his ill mother, of the kind lady who had given him lemon cakes and a riddle.

Still, a part of him wanted to impress Elizabeth by being her shining knight.

Apparently, the day had arrived.

The rain was lighter and more of a mist. No, that wasn't creepy at all. Somewhere above, the moon was trying to poke through the dark clouds.

Shadows played over the trees as the figures beyond moved toward him. The headlights of the car played off the wetness of the road and lit up the scene, adding to the shadow-play.

The sword in his hand caught the light and glistened. What was he thinking? Was it destiny that this sword, of which he had no true providence of its origins, had come into his life? Why was it hidden in that wardrobe? Who had helped him find it and why wasn't there anyone to help him now? For all he knew, it had been a long-forgotten wall decoration that someone had simply made a game of hiding for some unknown reason.

A wonderful time to be thinking those thoughts with what he was facing.

His destiny was the family he had made with Elizabeth, and it was his duty to protect them.

Such as a knight of old.

Like the knights of the Round Table.

Like King Arthur and Lancelot.

And…

The sword.

It could have been his imagination, but the thing seemed to glow slightly.

Ahead of him, the shadow of the menace had two smaller shadows hunched down next to it, like huge dogs heeling to their master. As Lawrence got closer, he could hear a rasping wheezing sound coming from the large shadow. Like it couldn't take a full breath. It was huge, well over seven feet tall. Lawrence didn't let the size or the fact that he couldn't make out a single feature of the figure he was approaching deter him. Was it a man or a shadow, or both?

Or was it just a cold blackness that threatened his family against which Lawrence would do anything to protect?

But then the shadow spoke, and Lawrence froze in his tracks.

"Lancelot?" it asked, stopping itself, even retreating a step it appeared. "How? How have you survived all these years? Some magic of Merlin's?"

"Stay away from my family!" Lawrence shouted, the light playing off his face.

The shadow again stepped toward him. "No, not Lancelot. Just a scrap of his legacy waving a knife around."

He was part of Lancelot's legacy. Was it true?

He took a deep breath and leveled his blade. "Come and find out."

"Bah," the shadowed thing said as it reached and grabbed one of the creatures by the throat. "Where is the Pendragon cow you saw?"

The creature replied in a frightful screeching sound, it's one good eye fearfully looking away toward Lawrence, "Only one in there, Master."

The Shadow threw the creature away as if it was a rag doll. The creature hit the car they arrived in with a loud crack and fell to the ground not moving.

The Shadow turned its attention back to Lawrence and said, "Where is the Pendragon cow?"

Just then, Lawrence realized that the discarded creature had lied to the Shadow. Could it be that for some reason it was protecting Elizabeth?

Now it was surely his turn.

"I'm sorry, who? I don't know what you're talking about."

The Shadow roared.

The creature next to the Shadow moved away in fear.

"The Pendragon, where is she?" The Shadow began to move toward Lawrence. He was a good ten yards away.

Lawrence wished it was more like ten thousand...

Chapter Thirty-Four

John feared the worst.

He knew he should be close. The rain had let up somewhat and from past experience he knew that might not be such a good thing.

These demons could control the local weather around them somewhat to make things as nasty as they could, to give them any sort of edge.

He said under his breath, "Please don't let anything happen to my family."

Chapter Thirty-Five

The Shadow took a few steps toward Lawrence but stopped when it got a good look at what he had in his hands.

The Shadow said, "What is that little knife you're carrying? Something to butter your bread?"

Lawrence tried to sound braver than he felt, "Why don't you come and find out?"

"Do you think such a minor thing in the hands of a novice can do anything more that annoy me?"

"We'll see."

"Do you think it will stop me from finding the one with Pendragon blood and killing her? Mother may believe her death will trigger the return of her half-brother from wherever Merlin sent him but I only care that another limb has been lopped off that tree."

Lawrence could feel a trickle across his hands like cold water dripping across them. Whatever it was, he felt more confident that he had a chance to slow this creature down and give Elizabeth an opportunity to get her and their daughter away.

Chapter Thirty-Six

Elizabeth's heart ached. She wanted to run to Lawrence and stop him. Years ago, she had seen what this monster could do and would never forget what he had tried to do in the old smoke shop.

But she also knew that their daughter would not survive if something happened to her and Lawrence.

She started to unbuckle Angela from the car seat just as there was a loud crash of the creature being thrown to the car. She saw it outside the window slump onto the ground.

It surprised her that she felt pity for it. More surprising, it had tried to help them in the only way it could by covering for them. She had heard it lie to its master. It had seen her. And she saw it suffer for protecting her.

Even though she had despised it years earlier she understood why Uncle John had stopped her from taking its life back then.

Because of the creature's sacrifice, she understood it's master couldn't penetrate the umbrella of invisibility created by the snowflake charm. She pulled her daughter tightly to her.

She was amazed Angela hadn't made a sound and was actually slightly smiling in the faint light, reaching up to touch her mother's face.

A tear ran down Elizabeth's cheek and onto the baby's fingers as she said, "Sweet girl, let's stay quiet, shall we? We have to get out of here."

Chapter Thirty-Seven

Lawrence moved away from the car to draw the creature away, not sure what Elizabeth was going to do. She was a clever girl, that one. All he knew at that moment was he needed to buy her time.

Time she would need to survive and protect their daughter.

He looked at the shadow figure. "So, you're a momma's boy, eh? Her little lackey?"

The shadow stopped abruptly then stepped toward him.

"What did you say?" it growled and took another step forward. Then another. Lawrence had done exactly as he'd hoped, keeping the creature's focus on him.

Damn it. Now what?

If only…

His thoughts raced as the shadow advanced.

If only…

If only he was the man he wished he could be, the man he needed to be for his wife and daughter. If only he was some vestige of the fighter his ancestor Lancelot (really, was that true?) had been.

If only his parents hadn't died and left him alone, alone to cope with a world of people who took the quiet, distant boy into their homes only to send him to another when there was no real connection made.

If only...

Then a thought occurred that made him catch his breath.

Elizabeth.

His life, tragic in places as it had been, had brought him to the love of his life.

Correction: the loves of his life. There was nothing he would not do for his wife and child, even give up his own life.

It was his honor to protect them, his good fortune to have them in his life, his duty to keep them safe from all evil.

For them, he would sacrifice all.

Suddenly...

Lawrence felt something strange happen as a surge of energy pulsed through his arm into the sword. It could have been his imagination, but the blade seemed to glow. And in the glowing, he could almost make out symbols etched into the metal.

The Shadow stopped suddenly. It hesitated as it seemed to sense the energy surge.

Lawrence looked from the blade to the Shadow. His lips curved into a small smile, and he thrust the blade toward the thing and watched it flinch away.

He knew then what he had and that there was a slim chance that he might be able to do more than slow the creature down. He suddenly had a chance to do some harm and possibly even more.

Over the years, Elizabeth had told him how certain items held energy one could only refer to as magical. Although before that moment he had never seen such a thing himself, he knew the sword in his hands was special.

It was his.

It was his legacy.

Lancelot's legacy.

Armed with renewed confidence, Lawrence raised the sword, the energy he felt coursing through it like nothing he had ever experienced.

The creature stalked forward. "Lancelot-spawn, child of the betrayer of the King, you shall die."

"That will be quite enough from you," Lawrence said, trying to sound a bit braver than he felt.

Lifting its sword to bring it down on him, the creature advanced but Lawrence brought his sword up to protect himself.

The blades met in midair, and fireworks seemed to explode from them. Lawrence's sword glowed more as he brought the sword around to slice at the shadow before him. It barely nicked it, but the creature howled in pain and rage as a trail of smoky shadow seeped from the cut.

Lawrence pressed and stabbed forward but the shadow creature parried the blow and nearly managed to draw blood itself, but Lawrence rolled out of the way. The thing's blade struck the pavement and etched a deep gouge in the asphalt.

Lawrence spun to attempt to hack it at the knees but was blocked. However, when the swords collided, a bright flash of light blasted out and the creature of shadow was thrown back several feet to land heavier than any shadow should, and Lawrence was laid flat on the pavement.

It rose, shaking what should be its head. Apparently, the lightshow had confounded it somewhat more than Lawrence. It stumbled, confused, swinging the sword in hopes of hitting something.

Lawrence rose, a bit unsteady himself, while opposite the creature stumbled around shaking its head.

Thinking he might get an attack in while he had the chance, Lawrence advanced but as he did, the sword began to glow.

Nononononono

Sensing the light, the creature chuckled harshly and turned to squarely face him. Difficult to sneak up on someone holding a big glow stick.

The Shadow Knight said, swinging his large sword back and forth. "So, that's no trinket after all, which of the twelve swords are you, little toy? My mother has Excalibur in her possession as well as its bastard brother sword Forspillan already. I need another taste." The shadow lunged forward, swinging at the glowing blade.

Lawrence brought his blade up to deflect the blow. This time the creature was ready as the energy exploded around them.

"Mundbora."

"No wonder you're so powerful. Mundbora is the Lancelot blood sword." the Shadow said, advancing slowly. "When a sword returns to its life blood, it is at its best tapping into old magic."

"Your ancestor was a betrayer of the Pendragon and did not deserve such a gift. And you have no idea how to wield that power."

Lawrence knew then that he had nothing to lose and that he would not survive this conflict. But he would give his wife and child every chance to escape.

It was his duty.

His legacy.

Lancelot's legacy.

Mundbora.

Protector.

Chapter Thirty-Eight

Camelot The Past

"Lancelot."

"Gwen."

'You shouldn't be here," she said, looking around for any witnesses. The castle and countryside were in tumult over the theft of Arthur's sword by his best friend. There were several groups out looking for him as they spoke.

"Camelot isn't safe for you now. Everyone is talking about hunting you down for stealing Excalibur."

"Gwen, I swear to you, it wasn't me. Well, it was, but it wasn't, it--I don't know how to explain it that will make any sense or will absolve me in even being a part of this."

"Lance, I don't understand."

"It was Mordred."

"Mordred? But he's only a boy."

"A boy? More like a demon, much like that mother of his."

"What does Arthur's sister have to do with any of this? I still don't understand."

"My body, Gwen! They stole my body! And used it to steal Excalibur!"

"But how could they steal it? You're right here!"

"Here. Thanks be to God and to Galahad. If not for him coming to my rescue..."

"Where is he now?"

"I don't know. I will find him. But for now, I must find Arthur and seek to make amends."

"Not so fast, Lancelot."

"Arik."

Chapter Thirty-Nine

"Betrayer of Pendragon," the Shadow hissed.

Lawrence stepped back, keeping his sword between them as the Shadow advanced step-by-step and touched blades. Sparks flew at the brief glancing blows

Memories of the stories of the Knights of the Round Table flooded Lawrence's mind. And stories of Lancelot. Stories had been told, countless books had been written, and endless films had sought to tell and retell the legends.

His personal favorite was actually the cartoon from Disney. Followed by the movie *Excalibur*.

In all those versions, the details changed but Lawrence sought to goad the Shadow into more information, perhaps even revealing enough to attain the upper hand.

Unlikely, but-

"What are you talking about, monster? I never betrayed Pendragon. In fact, I heard it was his sister who connived her way into betraying the king."

The Shadow reared up and then brought his sword down in a fury. "Lies!"

Lawrence chanced a confident smile he did not feel within as he said, "Well, hello...Mordred."

The thing hissed.

Lawrence took a step forward. "Did I strike a chord there?"

Silence except for the raspy breathing of the thing before him.

"I remember one story that it was Mordred himself, excuse me, yourself, that betrayed Arthur and Camelot."

The rasping breath sent swirling trails of moisture in the chilling evening air.

Lawrence pressed what he hoped was his advantage and so pressed his luck by glancing toward the car where Elizabeth and the baby might still be hiding.

The Shadow's head whipped around to look as well and the rasping breath turned into a rough laughter.

"Well played, but now it's time for this game to end. There are three links to the Round Table that will meet their ends tonight. So sad for the child."

"Well, not really." And the Shadow Knight started for the car.

"No!"

Lawrence broke into a run and swung his sword at the menace.

"You will leave my family alone!" With that, he launched into a flurry of blows at the thing, blinding flashes of light illuminating the scene around.

Over and over there were roaring blasts and thunderous crackles as their blades met. The sound was deafening but Lawrence could see the Shadow through the bursts of light and with each blow the thing seemed to be gaining an edge.

Lawrence was getting tired. It was one thing to get lessons on how to fight with a sword but quite another for a scholar to wage an all-out battle against such a fierce foe.

Even bolstered by the knowledge of his ancestry, he knew he was no Lancelot and not enough of a match against Mordred.

All he could really do was hope to hold on and pray that the other was feeling the same.

It wasn't looking that way, however.

Mordred pressed his advantage and goaded Lawrence as he rained blow after blow of the descendent of Lancelot. "He stole Arthur's soul, you know. He stole Excalibur in the dead of night and fled. That's the reason Arthur ran like a child and had Merlin send him through time."

Lawrence hesitated just for a second. Did he hear this creature correctly… time travel?

"I have killed several of Lancelot's spawn over time, but you may be the purest blood so far. I wonder if I killed your parents?" he boasted.

"No!" Lawrence howled as he renewed his efforts against the shadowed beast in the form of a man.

Mordred laughed, "Good! Come at me!

Come and meet your demise."

Chapter Forty

Elizabeth stayed behind the car, hidden as much as she could while cradling a cooing Angela.

She tried to steal glances through the car's windows at her husband, her Lawrence, fighting the Shadow Knight.

He was as fearsome as he had been when he had attacked her and her aunt years ago, but she could see him clearer for what he was.

Not a demon but a man. A deadly man, to be sure, but still a man. And Lawrence was actually holding his own against the beast. Almost.

She saw her husband swinging the sword at the Knight and the energy blasts that resulted. She had seen magic energy before and knew the sword was much more than they ever expected.

Would it be enough?

Lawrence was tiring, she could see that. She looked in vain for signs of other motorists or someone to help.

She stood and looked down the road hoping to see her Uncle but saw nothing but dark emptiness.

Oh, where was her Uncle John?

Chapter Forty-One

John thought he must be close. There was something bright flashing from somewhere up ahead. At first, he thought it was lightning, but it was at ground level, not coming from the sky.

He pressed the accelerator a little harder. He had to get there.

The question was, what would he do when he did?

Chapter Forty-Two

Elizabeth needed to move.

Clutching Angela to her chest, she took a step away from the car and the battle beyond. She didn't want to look back, but neither could she bear the thought of running away and leaving him.

Perhaps together they could do it. Perhaps the progeny of Pendragon and Lancelot together could beat the Dark Knight.

Angela reached up just then to touch her mother's face.

Pendragon and Lancelot.

She turned back to look but all she could see was a ball of energy with booming thunder shaking the very earth as Lawrence hacked away at the Shadow Knight and the swords clashing.

Every time the blades met, the energy around the pair seemed to expand. Elizabeth felt a connection to the magic and through it, she felt Lawrence.

She felt him.

But could he feel her in return? She tried to project as much encouragement and love as she could.

Then it happened.

For a split-second, Lawrence looked her way as if he could feel her in that connection as well. He looked away from his fight to seek her out and for an instant their eyes met.

Mordred took advantage and raised his sword skyward from the ground catching Lawrence across his chest. The blood from the wound erupted into the night sky as Mordred laughed in triumph.

A loud mournful cry filled the air as Elizabeth screamed "No!"

The demon turned to her.

She froze.

Whatever strength Lawrence had left him as he dropped to his knees, his hands shaking as he clutched the wound on his chest and tried to maintain a grip on his sword.

The light he felt was fading, in both himself and the blade.

Mordred looked at him in disgust.

"You see now where love gets you? Now watch as I end the line of Arthur and Lancelot in one fell swoop."

Lawrence said in defiance, "No!"

"Oh, yes."

Elizabeth pulled Angela tightly to her chest and backed away from the car. The Shadow Knight advanced, raking the tip of his sword along the ground, causing sparks as it went.

Thoughts of running were quickly dashed when she heard low growls behind her. The hellish hounds were circling behind her.

They knew where she was! Why wasn't the snowflake charm protecting her and the baby? Was the monster's power just too strong now, or was her own fear and anguish keeping the magic from protecting them?

Suddenly, another hound appeared between her and the pack. The scarred one was blocking the others from attacking her.

"You dare defy me, hound?"

The thing whined hearing that but went back to growling to keep the others at bay. Elizabeth's act of mercy had probably cost this poor thing its life, but in its final moments there was at least some small chance at redemption.

She turned back to face the Shadow Knight coming around the car. The steam and smoke from the engine swirling around him, adding to the otherworldly look of him.

There was no escape.

A wicked, ragged smile showed on his face for he knew his victory was upon him. A low, throaty laughter bubbled from deep within.

In a perverse way, it was almost a giggle.

Elizabeth stood defiant, Angela making baby noises, oblivious to the impending doom facing them.

When there was still a chance, she should have taken Angela and run, she knew. But she couldn't leave Lawrence. And now...

The air was charged with a magical tinge. That could have been her imagination really, given the circumstances. From somewhere and everywhere there seemed to be a high-pitched whistling building.

Then she saw something to the right on the high ridge moving fast toward the demon.

Blinks and flashes of lights that radiated then coalesced into bright balls that burst with mini claps of thunder.

And suddenly, through the stars that sprinkled her vision, she could see perhaps a half-dozen people standing where the lights had been.

More enemies? Please let it not be so...

No, it was people leaping from the ridge toward the demon each holding something that glowed.

Charms. The demon hounds broke off from stalking her to rush forward and face the new enemy popping into the fray.

The Shadow Knight staggered back from the wave of magical energy, surprised by the sudden appearance of the charm bearers.

"Oh, goodie," he said, "Now this is a fight!"

Chapter Forty-Three

Camelot The Past

"I don't want to fight you, Arik."

"You betrayed the king, Lancelot. How could you?

"It wasn't me."

"I just heard you. You said-"

"I said it was Mordred controlling my body through some bewitchment of Morgana's."

"I'm sorry, sire, how am I to believe such nonsense?"

"I'm sorry, too."

The silence that followed was broken by the sounds of two swords being unsheathed.

Chapter Forty-Four

He had seen a flash of light through the trees just past the next hill. John already had the pedal of the car pressed down as far as he dared. He wasn't slowing down until he had his family protected.

And fortunately, there weren't any turns coming up.

Except one!

The car slid around the corner and nearly off the road, but he corrected in time. Up ahead he could see their car askew on the road, steam or smoke rising from beneath the bonnet. Beyond there were several moving figures and in front one struggling to his feet but not making it, holding a...sword?

"No... please God." John whispered as he got his car back under control and slammed the brakes, sliding to a stop and illuminating the figure, bedraggled and bloody, using the sword to hold himself up.

Lawrence?

Past the damaged vehicle he could see a large shadowy being wielding a sword as well. Then he looked past the shadow and saw the monster and lights moving around it.

The lights emanating from other figures rushing toward the large one appeared to hurt the beast without really touching him. He staggered back but swung his sword wildly to keep them at bay.

"Where are Elizabeth and the baby?" John said out loud, confused at what he was seeing.

He opened his car door and started toward the shadows by Elizabeth's car. Pulling out the charm that his friend had given him many years ago just in case of this situation.

William warned him that the charm would kill the creature it was used against, but it also required something in return.

A life.

Elizabeth had seen the headlights of the car and wanted to run toward them, but the Shadow Knight still blocked the way. In her heart, she knew it must be-

"John!'

"Elizabeth!" John tried to get to his niece but was blocked from the scene by the battle raging between the Shadow thing and what he could see were hellhounds fighting at least half a dozen figures armed with charms such as his.

It was as bad as he had feared then. Worse, given the ferocity of the foe. Evil radiated from him as he fought on multiple fronts.

He had to get to Elizabeth and the baby, so he zigged and zagged as quickly as he was able, careful to avoid the conflict. And presently, he was with her. She collapsed into his arms, holding Angela tight.

John brushed the hair matted to her face by the rain away and said, "Are you hurt? The baby?"

She shook her head up and down as tears started streaming down her face. And pointed in the direction of where he had seen Lawrence.

All she could say was, "Lance".

John looked at the chaos of lights and heard the howls of the demon as if these tiny lights were causing it pain. If such a thing could feel pain. One of the attackers, a small older woman, reached beneath the demon's attack and got in one of her own. Mordred roared in fury and swatted her away.

John tried to move Elizabeth back to his car and away to safety. "Come, Elizabeth, we have to go... now, before it sees us."

She let him guide her a few steps and they found the way was blocked. He turned to look behind him and saw one of the hounds there, facing away from them.

As if guarding their backs?

Instinct more than anything caused John to duck, pulling Elizabeth with him as the Shadow Knight's sword swung over their heads.

He said, swinging the sword in a high arc, "You again. Will I never be rid of you do-gooders?"

There were few options left. John stood up and held the charm toward the beast.

A sacrifice to be made. A life to be given. He had had many years, had many adventures. And the two people behind him, mother and child, were two of the dearest things to him, the most precious. And worth whatever price needed to be paid.

The thing began laughing, "Thank you for being such a splendid target."

"Do your worst, villain."

"Nooo!" they heard, surprised by the sight of Lawrence, with the last vestiges of strength he had, leaping onto the hood of the car, using it to launch himself toward Mordred. His sword was poised to pierce the heart of the Shadow Knight.

Unfortunately, Mordred had a sword of his own waiting, and the two swords met their targets.

The look on Lawrence's face was one of triumph and yet, sadness. "You will not touch my family." And he pushed Mundbora deep into the shadows of Mordred's being.

The Shadow Knight staggered back, and Lawrence fell from the blade.

"You. Will. Not. Touch. My..." Lawrence said, as he sank to his knees.

Mordred was not to be denied such a prize of another death of the Round Table progeny, not when he was so close to victory.

Elizabeth was not ready to lose more and stood, defiant.

Then the baby Angela giggled, startling Elizabeth, her mirth in sharp contrast to the wretched doings going on around her. The giggle made her look down at her to see the baby pointing straight up at the sky.

Elizabeth looked up just as a figure flew over them holding two glowing charms, one in each hand. It landed between them and the knight. The figure crossed his arms and then pointed the charms at the creature, creating a blast that flung the beast over the car and beyond to land off into the ditch.

Mordred didn't move.

At first.

The hellhounds broke away from the fight to take up positions protecting their master. The one with the scar slinked away.

"Hurry...He is expecting you now." the figure said as he stood in front of the car protecting them from any other threats of attack for the moment. He was dark-skinned, a Native American from the States, she would guess from his accent and the stripes of paint across his cheek.

Elizabeth handed the baby to her Uncle. "I have to get Lawrence. I can't leave him here," she said.

John started to say something when the stranger reached from behind Elizabeth and put a hand on her shoulder. She turned and looked up at the man. He was much taller than her. Tears had started streaming down her face. She was angry and broken.

"You must go. He is waiting." Elizabeth started to interrupt but the man continued. "I promise we'll bring your husband home to you. Please, there is still danger."

She couldn't help it. She had to go to him She ran to where her husband lay. One of their protectors, the woman who had attacked Mordred earlier, cradling her husband's head in her lap and brushed the hair back from his face. Almost motherly.

She heard the woman say, "There, my brave knight, it will be all over alright."

Weak and dying, Lawrence managed to say, "Cordelia?"

"That's right, my boy, I lost you for so long! When I finally found you again, you were all grown up!"

"I th-thought you didn't want me." he said, tears mixing with the blood on his face.

She began to cry, "No, that was never the case. You were hidden from us for so long. We should have known others would want you for their own purposes. Lawrence, I'm so sorry I failed you."

Elizabeth stood above them, afraid to interrupt this newfound revelation.

Lawrence, his hand shaking, reached up to touch the woman's face.

"Did you ever get your family?"

"Yes, I married. And lost him, but I have a son. And guess what? He loves lemon cakes just as much as another little boy I once knew."

"I see you found your sword."

"I think I lost it again, but for a good cause."

"It took me a long time to figure that one out and a longer time still to find where that wardrobe was moved. Thankfully, we have people like Ling to help. She vowed to hold onto it for you. Her husband almost sold it a half-dozen times before you got there," she chuckled, although she found no humor in the moment.

Lawrence smiled and said, "It was a wonderful adventure. Elizabeth and I---where is Elizabeth?"

Lawrence looked up and saw Elizabeth above them. He held out his hand, which she took, sobbing.

"Elizabeth, meet Cordelia. Cordelia, meet the love of my life. One of them. The other is..." He tried to see past them to Angela.

"She's right here, lad," John said, bringing the baby around and holding her for her father to see and touch one last time.

Elizabeth's chest ached as she realized what this moment meant for her family, for her life, for them all.

"Is there nothing you can do, John?" she asked.

Her uncle could only shake his head sadly.

The Native American came up to the group. He said, "We must hurry. Rowan will help get you safe at home. The baby must be protected. She is the key to the final victory."

A roar behind them alerted them to the attack, a last effort from Mordred, Mundbura still embedded in his chest.

A dark shape leapt past them as the hound with the scar took up a position between them all. It missed narrowly being skewered by Mordred's blade as he raged.

"Traitorous dog!"

The distraction allowed the Native American time to reach into his jacket pocket and extract something. He muttered some words and threw a small bag at Mordred.

There was a bright flash and a loud pop as Mordred suddenly vanished. His stunned hellhounds stood confused before limping away.

"Did you just destroy him?"

"No, miss, I merely managed to send him away for now."

John looked at him and asked, "Merlin's Gate?" He had heard William talking of such a thing in the past amid all the talk of charms and other magical items.

The dark-skinned man nodded.

Elizabeth erupted in anger, "You mean you could have done that the entire time? Before he-he-" She sank to her knees next to her husband and sobbed.

Angela reached to touch her mother's face once again. Lawrence reached up to touch the other cheek.

"It will all be f-f-fine, my love. Protect our girl, eh?"

"Oh, Lawrence, I-"

The Native American stood over them and said, "Had I used it earlier, Mordred could have stopped me. I had to wait until he was weakened. He is still a danger even now."

"Where is he?"

"Somewhere in the Himalayas. Hopefully, he won't make it back but he has managed to live this long.

Morgana will not take this well. We must get you away from here."

Elizabeth said, "Not without Lawrence. Perhaps he can still-"

"Elizabeth. Go." her husband said, weakly grasping her arm. "Take Angela and get away from here. I haven't long to-"

"No!"

"You were my greatest quest, my love. For a brief moment in time, I tried to be the brave knight you needed, that you both deserved."

"You were," she said as his hand fell away.

"Lawrence?" but there was no answer.

He was gone.

Chapter Forty-Five

Camelot The Past

"I didn't mean to."

"He gave you no choice, Lance."

Lancelot knelt at the body of his former companion, another life claimed because of Morgana and Mordred.

He prayed the same didn't hold true for Galahad.

A voice from the dark startled them, "What have you done now, Lancelot?"

"Merlin!"

The mage stepped forward from the shadows which seemed to flow off him as if made from water. He looked down onto the body of Arik, Lancelot's bloody sword the answer his question.

"Ah, the boy. Sad."

"Is that all you can say, Merlin? His was a life of value, even if-"

"Even if Morgana had no hand in her grand schemes? Even now, her dark influence is at work. All of Camelot is against you, thanks to her."

"Well, almost all. My queen?"

Guinevere looked from Lancelot to Merlin, "What?"

"You can't be here, milady. Neither of you should be," the wizard said. He reached into his robes and took out a small bag.

Handing it to Lawrence, he said, "You know the words."

"But not the destination."

"Far from here. For now. Evil things are happening in the land and I need to get you somewhere safe."

"But Guinevere-"

Merlin held up a ringed hand to stop him, "will be safe at a nunnery I know of. The sisters will protect her."

"Merlin...I didn't want any of this to happen."

"Do you believe any of us did, boy? Now, get ready. You will be safe for the time being but when things are sorted out, you will be hunted, by the good and the bad."

"Especially the bad. You got away from her before but now, she'll burn the land trying to find you."

"She has Galahad. He saved me when Mordred took over my body."

Merlin paused and appeared to smell the air as he looked up into the night sky. "Galahad will be saved. I can say or see no more."

Lancelot grabbed hold of the wizard by the arms, "Do you swear? Will he be saved?"

Merlin looked pointedly down at the bloody hands upon him, causing Lancelot to step away.

"It may take some time, but for now, just remember Hollyhocks."

"Now is no time to talk about flowers!"

"That is your destination, dolt. There is a cottage in the north country where you can lay low for now and regain your strength. Now, away with you. I must take care of this particular mess because once you use that magic, there will be some unwanted attention and I would rather be left to deal with it."

Lancelot looked once more at Arik's body. Then at Guinevere, struggling for the words he needed to say.

Merlin interrupted him, "Now would be a good time. Hell has frozen over, and things are going to get heated around here."

"Merlin…"

"Seriously, Lancelot you must hurry and be away! Why won't you understand?"

Lancelot held the bag in his hand and nodded. "Will Camelot suffer?"

"You mean Arthur? Yes, I'm afraid he will. But your progeny will win the day. I hope."

"What do you mean-" Merlin held up his hand again and pointed to the bag.

"Now."

Lancelot nodded and recited the words Merlin had taught him and ended with Hollyhocks. And with a bright flash and a pop, he was gone.

Guinevere staggered back, not believing her eyes. Merlin approached her and handed her a small bag of dirt and looked her in the eyes. "My Queen, you must be away as well. However, in your condition, I fear what this will do to your health."

"My condition? I don't-"

"Please, Guinevere, I haven't the time. I know that you and Arthur will have a child. People will lie and say it's Lancelot's, but people are fools. You are not. Take care and repeat these words after me. Now hurry, I hear the voices of the guard."

And soon she was gone as well, leaving Merlin with the body. He doused it with a vial of diluted demon's blood taken months before from Lancelot's clothing then tossed a bag onto the body as he recited the incantation that would whisk him away.

The men of the guard came soon after to find Merlin alone sprinkling powder around that flashed and burned in the air.

"Milord Merlin, we saw some lights this way and heard some frightful noises."

Merlin dusted his hands off and smiled. "My fault, I'm afraid. I was setting upwards to keep demons away. Those noises may have been some nearby setting off my traps."

"D-demons?"

"Oh, yes, nasty ones. Smell that?"

The men looked at each other, concerned, and backed away. One said, "I smell it."

"Me, too."

Merlin pointed down the path away from them, "If there were any, they would be that way. Or.."

"Or?"

"Or you could wait until morning. They don't like the light much, you see. Hence, the flashes."

The men nodded and made to go back the way they came.

"Sounds reasonable. We'll leave you to it, milord."

And Merlin was once again, alone.

"Yes, reasonable."

There was work to do.

Chapter Forty-Six

Elizabeth had her Uncle sit in the passenger seat of the car he had driven and hold the baby while she installed the baby's car seat from their car.

The protectors canvassed the scene, making sure there were no more threats. The hellhound with the scar had disappeared along with the others but she doubted it would return with them.

She said to the Chief (as she had come to think of him), "You had better keep your promise and bring him home to me."

The man stood tall with his arms crossed, the charms glowing. He looked at her and nodded. Very slowly, he said "I will. Cordelia will make sure of it. She's wounded but she insists on being with him."

Elizabeth refused to cry more. At least, not then. She put the baby in her car seat, then went around to the driver's side and got in.

John said, "Elizabeth, you're upset. Let me drive you."

"Are you mental? We've already nearly died once tonight."

"Hmph."

And with that she drove down the lane, leaving behind the life she had imagined. Plans for the future were already racing through her mind.

"No more will die, John. I have to protect them."

And in the backseat, baby Angela soon fell asleep.

Chapter Forty-Seven

Days later, there was a ceremony for Lawrence at her grandfather's bee farm. There were several of the charm bearers in attendance, including the Chief and Cordelia.

Around a great oak table in her grandfather's study, they all gathered. She smiled when she realized the shape in the context of the company she was keeping of late.

She was making plans. All traces of the Snowflake Codex had been removed from the University. Vice-Chancellor Justin had been invaluable in that effort, privately assisting but publicly disparaging the use of the University's resources.

Using the Codex, Elizabeth would help protect the bloodlines of Camelot. She vowed to find a way to destroy the monster, his mother, and any others who might threaten her family, new and old.

The bloodlines were her family now and she would do whatever it took.

No more death.

Her grandfather had been researching the swords of Camelot. Legends said there were twelve swords, but he could only trace back ten.

Of course, the one that everyone knew was Excalibur, the fabled sword of Arthur which was in the hands of Morgana according to Mordred.

But there were others, including Lancelot's Mundbora that Lawrence had found in the wardrobe in the antique shop. They had last seen it sticking out of Mordred before he was magically sent away.

She vowed they would find it again. It was now Angela's legacy as well.

The baby sat in the lap of Cordelia delighting those around her. A charmer, much like her father.

Her grandfather believed the swords might be the key to beating evil. They may be the strongest charms that exist.

She disagreed. Love and family was the strongest charm they had going for them.

He knew better than to argue with her.

Chapter Forty-Eight

Elizabeth stood in the middle of a field looking toward the ocean. The land was beautiful.

Angela was running around with her Uncle. At two years old she was proving to be an adventurous soul in spite of having been in such danger the year before. She tugged on her Uncle's hand, dragging him to the next large stone that jutted out of the ground and he was doing his level best to keep up with her.

Just barely.

"This is a true dead zone for magic," Eizabeth said aloud.

Much like the snowflake charm and the other magical charms but on a far grander scale, her grandfather had said.

He had added that for whatever reason, something happened there, and magic wouldn't work.

Good enough, she thought.

That was the reason the Chief was standing back by the car down the lane. Just outside of the area. Watching for anyone and anything that shouldn't be there. He was now with them much of the time, although at times he disappeared back to the states to attend to things there.

There were others now as well, including the charm bearer Rowan and his squad, but the Chief had excelled in learning the skills of the charms and bringing the old knowledge of the American Indians that was shared with him as a child of a tribal shaman. He was becoming a very powerful shaman and protector himself.

Elizabeth felt it. This was the place to start over.

To the west were mountains and caves and to the east was a small town. Her grandfather had started buying up the homes. He wanted every square inch of the magical dead zone.

Toward the ocean were some remains of a castle. The locals believed it was Camelot of course. The rumors were that just about every castle ruins were that of Camelot. The odds were highly likely that these were but some small ocean post to protect from invaders from the water. That meant something around here was important enough to protect.

To the south a couple of miles was a military base.

There were trees, excellent oaks, where Angela was running with John not far behind, winded but still there. Ever-vigilant, ever-doting.

Her Grandfather and Uncle pulled a few strings to acquire the property from the owners and now it was theirs.

No more will die.

New Camelot would be a sanctuary for everyone they could find.

Camelot would rise again, she thought as the sun was setting on the ocean.

Tomorrow it will begin.

Elizabeth laughed as Angela gave one of the hugest of trees a fierce hug and no amount of coaxing from John could get her to let go.

Funny that, the tree looked for all the world as if it had a face.

And the face was smiling.

Epilogue

America

The Chief ducked as he entered the cavern where he was expected. Long ago torches had lit the way, but at present solar-powered lights illuminated the passageway as well as the huge cavern.

"How do things progress across the waters?" his grandmother asked as he emerged into the great underground hall. She was halfway around the cave on a sturdy steel walkway that had long ago replaced one of timbers and rope.

"They show promise. She shows great promise."

"As do you. "

"You honor me, grandmother, even as you continue to teach me more of the world's mysteries."

"But I come bearing gifts. More bags of dirt."

She laughed, "Just what I hoped for."

A familiar voice spoke from the shadows, "And I trust you said the words I taught you the way I taught you."

"Of course."

The figure stepped forward, the shadows running off him as if made of water. Below them on the cavern floor was a map of the world across the expanse, the largest of the Merlin's Gates in the New World, ready to be used. The bags of dirt from the grounds just outside New Camelot would come in handy.

"Good. Let's get to work."

###

A Special Gift

Thank you for reading Camelot Forever Lancelot's Redemption. The story continues in Camelot Forever Pendragon's Return.

As a special gift we have included the story Camelot Forever Snowflake by Robert W Hickey and Bill Nichols. Snowflake tells the story of a young Elizabeth and the adventures that lead to Camelot Forever Lancelot's Redemption.

Camelot Forever

Snowflake

A prequel to
Camelot Forever Lancelot's Redemption

Robert W. Hickey & Bill Nichols

Camelot Forever: Snowflake copyright 2021 Bobby Hickey All Rights Reserved.
Camelot Forever logo is ™ 2021 Bobby Hickey.

Camelot Forever: Snowflake was edited by Bill Love and Wendy Love

Before...

December 24th, Christmas Eve south of London, England.

"Auntie, I found it!"

The young girl raced down the hallway of the small apartment, careful to not trip on the old green rug in her haste...again...as she rushed to show her aunt the treasure she had just re-discovered.

"Aunt Anne?"

From the hallway closet, the woman she sought emerged, burdened with their coats and scarves to brave the cold outside.

"Found what, dear?" her aunt asked. Somewhere in her sixties, she smiled broadly at this wonderful blonde child who continued to brighten her days, especially when the days of late had been so dark.

She peeled off a red child-size coat and a bright white scarf to hand her.

The young girl of ten, stood in front of her aunt, proudly presenting her find. "My ornament! It's the one Uncle George would always tell me was my mother's."

The older woman reached out as the girl placed it into her hand as if it were a delicate flower just blooming with the promise of spring. She carefully regarded the ornament, and yes, it was indeed that old ornament.

To some it might simply look to be an old glass ball, some of the paint at the top and bottom just beginning to flake off with age.

But inside the glass ball, a small silver snowflake hung so when light shone through the ornament, it created a sparkling shadow effect quite unlike anything Anne had ever seen.

With the corner of her woolen scarf, she dabbed away a tear before handing the ornament tenderly back to her niece.

"Your Uncle George indeed loved his younger sister very much. He and your mother were quite the pair, I must say. Always caught up in the old stories. And now…"

"Well, I know the two of them are watching over us." The woman caressed the girl's cheek and smiled. So much like her mother. And yet still so much like her late father without ever having known either, losing them at such a young age.

Still, she was going to be a force to be reckoned with when she grew up, no doubt.

The girl stared intently at the snowflake shadows playing within the orb, rapt with wonder, a wide smile across her face. The very image of her mother when she had been that age.

"Go hang it on the tree, Elizabeth, then get your coat and things on. We must get the shop opened. It's Christmas-time and we shall have a great many customers stopping by for gifts today!"

"Yes, ma'am," Elizabeth answered as she dashed to the Christmas tree and hung the ornament revernantly in the middle of the tree.

If Anne's camera had been handy, the image of the girl bathed in the lights of the tree as she admired her mother's snowflake ornament would have been one to cherish.

The image was dashed as the girl broke out into a run and fled down the hallway.

"Oh, wait, I must find a book!"

Yes, Anne smiled, so very much like her mother.

Elizabeth emerged from her room brandishing her latest find, a story book about knights and dragons. Again, she narrowly avoided tripping over that cursed green rug, but she recovered quickly, almost gracefully.

Anne said "Haven't you read that one already?"

Elizabeth grinned, "Yes, but the adventures they all had makes it all worth reading again and again!"

"Hm, then how about something new? I believe we could make an exception this once and allow you to open, say, one present early? Hm?"

The girl's jaw dropped open and her eyes gleamed. "Yes!" she exclaimed.

"Then have at it, my love. Which shall it be?"

The girl raced to the presents scattered under the tree. "I know just the one!"

She came back clutching a gift wrapped in red paper with a green ribbon and bow. "This one!"

"Are you certain?"

"It's a book, I just know it!"

"Let's see, shall we? Perhaps it's a cookbook! Or one about penguins!"

"Oh, Auntie..." Elizabeth said as she tore at the end of the present and indeed slid a book out the end of the paper.

It was a book of the adventures of a great detective from a hundred years ago. Holding it away from her, she stared at it for several seconds, not uttering a word.

"Well?" her aunt said, "Does it suit you?"

The girl's face erupted in a greater smile than before answering "Oh, yes."

"Who was it from, by the way?"

"I almost forgot to look in my excitement!" Elizabeth turned the paper over and looked at the name on the tag.

"Uncle George? And you?"

"Yes, he found that a few weeks before he...passed. He just knew no matter where he hid it, you would find it. You are quite the detective yourself."

She threw her arms around her aunt and said, "I love it."

Anne said, hugging the girl fiercely in return, "George would be so pleased. Now, we had better scoot! We have things to do!"

Elizabeth said as she put on her coat. "I miss Uncle George."

"So, do I, my girl," the older woman said as she held the door open for her niece before leaving the apartment.

As the door closed, she caught a last glimpse of the ornament on the tree and the wrapping paper on the floor and swallowed hard.

"Very much," she whispered.

Chapter One

Stepping out on into the street, a strong cold wind hit Elizabeth, making her pull her scarf around her ears to stave off the blast of bitter cold.

She grabbed her aunt's hand with one hand, her new book clutched in the other, as they hurried along the sidewalk.

"Auntie, do you think it's going to snow this Christmas?"

"The weatherman says we could very well have a white Christmas. You know, it all starts with just a single snowflake," her aunt replied. "Would you like some pastries from Jackson's Bakery before we open up the shop?"

"Yes, please! I love Mr. Jackson's pastries and I sort of forgot to eat breakfast looking for my ornament."

"What am I going to do with you, my sweet pea? Now, we only have a few extra minutes, so we'll just run in and pick a few of his very best!"

Elizabeth laughed, "But they're all so good, how can there be a very best?"

Neighbors waved as they passed on this cold, cold day. The wind had picked up, fierce and biting as the two moved up the side toward the little smoke shop they owned.

"It's colder than a witch's heart out here this morning," mumbled the older woman as she dragged her young niece along the street.

As they passed a few store fronts Elizabeth stopped in front of the television repair stop next to the bakery. In the large front window several tellies were on display, each hooked to a different VCR, playing a different Christmas movie .

"Oh, look! White Christmas!" exclaimed Elizabeth. "That's my absolute favorite Christmas movie. May I please watch it while you get our pastries?"

"Don't you want to say hello to Mr. Jackson?"

"Please, Auntie?"

"Don't you want to help pick them out? You always choose the very best ones, you know."

"Auntie, you can do it. You know they are the very best."

"Well, if you say so…"

"Especially if it's blueberry…"

"Well now, you see, I would never have known that. I might have picked out a nice rhubarb pie for you."

The girl put her hands on her hips and stood her ground as she said, "No, you wouldn't have. You know very well what I like."

The older woman's laughter rang through the air. "Yes, that is true."

"All right, but you must stay right here and do not move." Anne said. She was apprehensive about leaving her alone, if only a storefront away, but she knew that with her husband gone she would need Elizabeth to be more independent, to take on more responsibility for herself, at school and helping at the shop. Never having children of her own, she knew she had a problem letting this precious child go. One day, all too soon, she would be all grown up and making all sorts of decision of her own.

She would be fierce. And no time like the present to start her on that road, perhaps.

"I won't move," Elizabeth promised.

"See that you don't, young lady," said her aunt as she entered the bakery. The bells on the door jingled as she entered and was greeted by Mr. Jackson.

The wonderful smells of the bakery reached Elizabeth and her stomach began to growl. Through the window, she could hear her aunt, still glancing her way before stepping further into the shop to greet Mr. Jackson. His loud joyful voice was full of sincere excitement. always ready to share in the local gossip with a neighboring shop owner.

Elizabeth suspected they would be opening the smoke shop a little late today.

As she returned to watching the Christmas movie buffet in the repair shop window, she suddenly noticed a person sitting on the pavement at the corner of the next shop past the bakery.

Curiously, he hadn't been there before. Had he? She?

The person was covered in several coats, hoods, and blankets. A small tin can, its label once proudly sporting a picture of some vegetable, sat next to the person. A few coins lay near it, most likely from folks who wanted to drop them in but didn't deem it too necessary to get too close.

She took a step toward the person, knowing her aunt had told her not to move but it was only on the other side of the bakery so it should be okay. Technically, she was still in view...

She put her new book on the ground where she stood as if to mark her place, or else give her a spot to retreat to if necessary.

Elizabeth then walked up the the person, wondering if the person was even alive given how cold it was outside. Could he have frozen in the middle of the night?

Perhaps one of her Auntie's blizzard goblins she threatened her with when she left a door or window open had frozen the person and left them as a block of ice as a warning to others on the streets.

Just then a puff of steam came from somewhere around the head of the person. Ah, good, he was alive, at least. The puff seemed to shift slightly in mid-air then move toward her, as if tracking her. It reminded her of a dog, the way it almost appeared to sniff her out.

Surely her vivid imagination was at play here...

Not knowing if it was a man or woman Elizabeth decided to simply offer to help pick up the coins and place them into the can. And then retreat to her former post in front of the Christmas movies.

"Hello, how are you today?" Elizabeth said as she got closer.

No answer came.

"Hello? I see that you have a few coins that missed your collection can."

Still no answer.

"Um, hello there, if you wanted, I could help you get them in the can." With no answer still, Elizabeth knelt to pick up the coins, but a wave of the most horrific smell wafted over her. Like nothing she had ever smelled before, it almost made her get sick to her stomach.

She thought to just back away from the person, but remembering her manners, she didn't say a word and knelt back again to pick up the coins.

"I'm-I'm just going to put them-" she started to say when she heard something. Whatever it was, it didn't sound like a voice or even human, but more like an animal. Then it died away.

Looking around, she picked up the first coin and dropped it into the can. The sound seemed to be much louder than it should.

With only the two other coins, she thought she could easily help this person and get back to her Christmas show before her aunt came out.

As she started to pick up the second coin, she found it sticking to the ground. Some kind of goo trailed from the coin like melted cheese as she moved it to the can.

"This one's a bit of mess, but-" As the coin dropped from her, tiny tendrils of something awful trailing it, a gnarled hand shot from the blankets and grabbed her wrist.

A mighty scream was building within Elizabeth when suddenly she heard the animal noise again. This time she could make out words.

"What's your name, girl?"

She replied "Elizabeth"

"No, child, your surname?" quickly replied from the bundle of blankets from which the dirty wrinkled hand protruded.

She replied, defiant, "LeoDegrance".

"I don't recognize it," crackled the sound from somewhere within the piles of blankets. The hand pulled her closer and the horrible smell was worse.

"My-my uncle owned the smoke shop on the next block," she said as she turned her head and veered her nose away.

"Old George, eh? Well, you don't say." The hand released her, and she quickly stepped back a few steps.

"Died of the Big C a few months back, did he not?

"Sort of funny the thing that feeds your family is what kills you, eh?"

Elizabeth took offense at this and yelled, "There's nothing funny about my uncle dying."

"Of course not. Dying just happens." a reply came. "Happens all the time."

"Besides my aunt's closed the testing room so we no longer have the smoke in the shop. So-" "At the sound of the little bells on the bakery door, Elizabeth turned to see her Aunt leaving the bakery, balancing a box of pastries.

Her aunt was saying in an over-loud voice to the baker inside, "I'll be sure to tell her that you saved her favorite, a nice rhubarb tart just for her on Christmas Eve."

She turned to see if Elizabeth had heard the joke just as the girl ran to her and grabbed her arm, pulling her away.

"Come on, Auntie, we're going to be late opening the shop!"

Something in the way Elizabeth was acting, as if she might be a little scared, caused the woman to look around for some possible danger.

But there was nothing. Only the book she had just gotten as a gift placed neatly on the sidewalk in front of the television repair shop.

The two passed the corner where the person was, and nothing was there. Not a person, blankets, can or even the coin that was covered in goo.

Everything was gone.

Elizabeth stopped and was puzzled. Had she imagined it all? She had only turned away an instant.

No one could have moved that fast.

Anne stopped and looked at her. "Elizabeth, is something wrong? You're behaving a bit strangely. Perhaps it was a bad idea leaving you alone out here. The world is a most dangerous place and you'll be on your own one day..."

With one last look around, Elizabeth shook her head and answered, 'No, I'm fine, Auntie. Let's go open the shop."

"Then come along, my girl, the aroma of these pastries are giving me hunger pangs."

"Me, too!"

The two started off, but Elizabeth suddenly broke away to retrieve her book. One last look around, and she joined her aunt.

Chapter Two

On Cobden Street, only a few streets to the east from Elm Street where George and Ann's smoke shop was located, a solitary figure shuffled down the shadowed sidewalk.

Unlike Elm where all the storefronts were lit up from streetlamps, Cobden had no streetlights shining at all. The lampposts that were still standing were either broken or else no one figured it was worth the bother replacing the bulbs.

Several of the store fronts had long been boarded up, the owners and customers forgotten and abandoned.

Many of the windows and been broken out and graffiti had been sprayed on the walls inside and outside of the buildings.

Gentrification would not reach this area for some time, if ever.

From there, one could just barely hear the Christmas music playing from the old St. Mark's Church on the corner of Elm and 19th Street. They always played the holiday music to get those within hearing distance into the Christmas spirit.

The shambling figure mumbled to no one but itself and kept repeating: "It's his. It's his." in some Celtic crackling pitched animal sound.

The figure turned down an alley shrouded in shadow. Nothing stirred here, not the wind or even a rodent. Nothing except the figure who continued to repeat itself.

The figure continued down the alley, moving as if it didn't need light to see. Then it turned into another alley, then stopped at a faded wooden door.

Pressing a wrinkled hand against the frame, strange Celtic words were whispered. Glyphs glowed on the portal and the old door opened with a creak.

The figure moved through a large dusty warehouse toward a small office in the far corner. Inside a single light glowed, barely illuminating a man at a large old desk.

"What do you want, Hound?" the man said as the figure stumbled into the office, using the same Celtic broken language.

"It's him. His blood. It's his. It's his" whispered the figure. "I touched her to make sure."

"Him who, Hound? Gaheris, Orkney or Lamorak? Now that knight sired so many bastards, he filled half of the lands with his bloodline."

The figure hesitated before answering, then said, "The Dragon."

The man sat back in his chair, laughing cruelly, mocking. "Oh, The Dragon, you say? Well, did you now?

"Do you know how many Hounds come running in here and tell me they have found the bloodline of Pendragon?"

The figure said nothing, only barely backed away from the man at the desk.

The man continued. "The master has placed such a high reward on this everyone is wanting to claim the prize."

The figure still said nothing.

"The funny thing, Hound, is that not one of them has actually found the Dragon."

He leaned forward, "Not. One."

From somewhere else in the building came screams and sounds of pain and agony. The cruel eyes of the man watched the pathetic figure before him as he said

"The last demon that came in here saying he had found the Pendragon, claiming the reward, well, it obviously didn't work out well for him. So, I've decided to stop wasting my time and any Hound that comes in and falsely tries to claim the prize will be tortured. Do you know how you torture a demon Hound?"

The figure nodded slowly.

"I thought you might. Now, think carefully before you answer: Who do you think it was you found?"

In a low voice, the figure answered, "It's him. The Pendragon's bloodline. It's his. It's his."

The man shook his head, as if sad. "Oh, Hound, I suppose you'll be next."

The figure stood its ground.

"Tell you what. I haven't had a snack today. Why don't you stick around while I go to prove your find? Then you can claim the prize." The man laughed as he stood and came around the desk. At that, the Hound retreated a few steps toward the corner of the room.

But the rather large man reached down and picked up a large red coat with white trim around the collar and cuffs. As he pulled on his suspenders and pulled the coat on he asked the Hound, "Where is my snack, Hound?"

"Old George Smoke Shop on Elm. A little girl," crackled the figure.

"Ho, Ho" shouted the large figure in red as he exited the building. "A mere morsel. Good thing I'm not really hungry then. Now, stay put, Hound. I'll be back to give you your punishment directly."

The figure stood stock still and merely whispered over and over,

"It's his. It's his."

Chapter Three

"Holmes, we must be moving along if we're to make it to London by Christmas. I can't believe you're leaving your precious bees for a evening out on the town." said an older gentleman dressed with a proper suit and hat straight from the 30's.

"My dear Watson, you truly didn't expect me to not join you on this adventure, did you?" replied William, a tall man in a black suit.

"Well, you did suggest we get out on the town a few weeks ago and you know how I love the holidays."

"Yes, Watson, I do indeed."

The two men climbed into the back of a limousine and William told the driver to take them to Old Brixton.

"Old Brixton? Why are we going there? It's 30 miles south of London!" said Watson.

"John, I believe we need one more adventure," William said as he settled in for the hour ride.

"I don't think your idea of adventure and mine are the same, Holmes. Just what is it you're dragging us into?

"And why the limousine?"

"Who is to say we can't have an adventure in style?"

"Now, settle in. And since we have a bit of a ride ahead I'll explain what I've been doing since I've become a beekeeper. Do try not to nod off, won't you?"

"Who, me? Perish the thought."

"Well then, Watson. You know I've been studying the advancement of DNA science...are you snoring?"

"No, of course not. Just resting my old eyes."

"Well then, as I was saying..." The car sped off as the two old friends discussed bees as well as past and possible future adventures.

As they had for much of the past hundred years.

Chapter Four

The morning had been a flurry of customers. Many people needed a last-minute gift for a loved one. Thankfully, Uncle George had pre-ordered many gift sets in advance of the approaching holiday season.

And so, it was just past 2:30 when Elizabeth finally walked out the door of the shop and headed down to Mr. Jackson's Bakery to get her Aunt and herself a sack lunch, usually a fresh bagel with whatever special spread Mr. Jackson had made, often ham salad, a bag of crisps and a freshly made cookie.

"Elizabeth don't let Fred keep you. I need you back before the next rush of customers. And please be careful," her Aunt called after her.

"You know he gets lonely after lunch time, Auntie. No one buys pastries in the afternoon until he drops the price near closing time. Besides, he loves to tell stories about the old days."

"Just get back here quickly, Sweet Pea."

Elizabeth replied "Yes, ma'am," as she closed the door behind her and started walking down the street.

She stopped at the corner where she had the strange encounter earlier in the morning and stared at the empty space. She remembered how bad the person in rags smelled and the strange way he talked. It was unlike anything she had ever heard or smelled before. It was almost upsetting her stomach just thinking about it now.

Then she heard a voice call her. Mr. Jackson.

"Ah, Elizabeth," the short fat man stood half-way out the door beckoning her in. So wrapped up in her memories of the morning's strange encounter, she hadn't even heard the jingle of the bells on the door.

"Your aunt said you were on your way to pick up a couple of lunch sacks. I was worried you may get lost. I made a ham salad just for you."

"My favorite!" cried Elizabeth as she skipped toward the bakery, as youthful and happy as any ten-year-old girl would be on Christmas Eve.

Mr. Jackson had kept her much longer than Aunt Anne would have wanted her to stay. Her aunt had even called and told Mr. Jackson to send her back because she needed help.

Mr. Jackson offered to close up the bakery early to come help Anne for a bit even though he might be busy himself with customers picking up last- minute holiday cookies and pies, as well as Elizabeth's favorite, Christmas Cake. She loved all the candied fruit inside. Yummy!

She hoped her aunt would have one for them to share tomorrow after they unwrapped presents.

As she finally left the bakery, lunch sacks in hand, she looked up the block to see someone dressed as Santa Claus leaving the smoke shop. He seemed happy, almost skipping as he walked, a strange sight for such a large man.

As she approached him, she heard a sound like he was humming a song, although it wasn't any song that she recognized. Actually, it did sound more like humming but there was something else.

She walked right up to him and waved, "Hello, Santa."

The man stopped and did something rather strange. He appeared to sniff the air and then looked down right at her.

She had seen someone else sniff the air earlier.

Santa replied, "Why, hello, little girl." He pulled off his gloves to show old, wrinkled hands as he reached into a box and pulled out a cookie.

"Would you like a cookie?" She recognized the box from Mr. Jackson's bakery.

"Yes, I would, but...I haven't had lunch yet," replied Elizabeth.

"Ah, well, yes, no need to spoil your appetite then. How about keeping it for later, for dessert?"

Santa held out the cookie to her. Yes, she could save it for later, even share with her aunt. As she reached for the cookie, Santa clutched her hand.

The man jumped back as if he had been shocked, even dropping the box of cookies and mumbling something Elizabeth couldn't quite make out. But it sounded eerily familiar, it sounded the same as the ragged person.

"Oh no, Santa, you dropped your cookies!" replied Elizabeth as she knelt to pick them up for him.

The man just stared at her the whole time that she picked them up, not offering to help, just standing there as if he was in shock.

"Are you alright?" Elizabeth said.

Santa's voice cracked as he shook himself, "Oh my, my, my, yes, my dear. This is indeed a day for gifts."

"Well, then, here you are." Elizabeth smiled hesitantly as she handed the box of cookies back to the Santa, then walked into her aunt's shop with their lunch bags.

The Santa continued to simply stand there and watch her every step as she went. Underneath the fake white beard and Santa hat, something was smiling.

Something very nasty, something not so nice.

Chapter Five

The limousine pulled in front of a charming old pub called The Pink Lady and the two gentlemen stepped out the back.

The sounds of Christmas music played from just around the street corner. William informed the driver they would contact him when they needed to be picked up.

John watched the car pull away and said, "How is he supposed to know when we need to be picked up?"

"I'll call him."

"How?" replied John.

William laughed "He has a phone in the car, old man, get with the times."

John just stood there and shook his head and said. "Wonders of a modern world...What's next? Will we be carrying phones in our pockets as well?"

"Sooner than you think, my old friend."

The two entered the pub and found a corner table. William always preferred his back against a wall, so he wouldn't be distracted and that no one could walk up behind. It always made for better outings.

"John, as we spoke back in the car, I have tracked down someone who needs our protection. I need to retrieve an item and I need to to check out the surroundings to see if any of LeFay's hounds are around."

"Dash it all, Holmes. I'm retired from all this stuff."

"You're as retired as much I am a beekeeper. This is one person we have to protect."

"Just like that little Indian girl back in the 40's that we had to save."

"She was important but this one is the last of her line." rebutted William. "For now."

Chapter Six

A white Bentley, looking severely out of place for the area, pulled down Cobden Street before turning down a familiar alley. A large delivery door opened on the back of a building and the car pulled inside.

A large powerful figure climbed out from the driver's side. The man was wearing a nice three-piece suit that looked as though it could barely contain his large frame. A shadow figure bundled in rags approached, but not too close.

"Where's Moog?" the figure growled. The shadowy figure pointed toward the tiny office with the glowing light.

The man stalked across the warehouse floor, stirring swirls of dust in his wake with each stride. He barely fit through the doorway of the office and upon entering made the small office feel even smaller. "You sent a crow, Moog?"

Moog sat on the edge of his desk still wearing the Santa pants and holding the jacket. On the ground was the fake beard that he had dropped. The creature looked up at the figure, a look of awe on his face.

"Master... it's his blood. The one that you seek."

The figure replied "You said the old man was the first in years and the last, since he had no children. Even then you took care of him yourself, so why bring me out here?"

"He was already sick, but this one, she is special. I touched her and there's something I can't explain, Master."

"You had better- and quickly, before I crush you and this hive of cockroaches you have here."

"Yes, Master."

Outside the office, figures gathered from the shadows and chanted in whispers, "It's his. It's his."

Chapter Seven

The day had indeed been very busy. Aunt Anne was just starting to clean the stop as closing time approached.

Mr. Jackson had stopped in after closing the bakery and dropped off a box for her Aunt which she believed might be her Christmas Cake as well as a present for her which she wasn't allowed to open until Christmas day.

His face lit up when she had told him how good the ham salad had been. He had smiled and listened as she told him about her new book and her love for Christmas Cake. He chanced a look and a quick wink to her aunt at that.

After he left with a hardy Merry Christmas! Elizabeth said, "I really like Mr. Jackson."

"He has always been such a good friend to your Uncle and me since we moved the shop here."

Elizabeth followed with "Was his wife alive then?"

"Yes, Martha was alive and they both spent much of their time in the bakery. She was always so busy after their daughter got married and moved to London."

"About four years ago she started to have some bad days. And then it got to be bad weeks. Fred was a mess. She seemed to get better but the next thing you know, she passed away."

"That's so sad." She watched out the window as Mr. Jackson disappeared down the street, waving at passers-by and wishing them all a Merry Christmas.

"Yes. With his daughter moved away and his wife gone Fred has made that bakery his life."

"Well, he makes really good ham salad, too."

"Yes, he does. Now you finish sweeping these floors and I'll restock the imports and we can go have our Christmas Eve dinner."

Anne went into the back stockroom as Elizabeth grabbed the broom and began to sweep

Just then, the door opened, and a rather large man entered the store. Elizabeth looked up and up and up at what must have been the tallest man she had ever seen.

He was dressed all in black and looked as if he had just walked out of some business meeting in his fancy suit. The man filled the small area in front of the display cases filled with imported cigars.

"May I help you?" she said as he stared down at her.

"Hm, the Pendragon's blood does indeed flow within you, girl," "I can smell its stench from here." the large man said at last.

His accent was much like that she had heard earlier today. His voice was more defined, yet somehow demonic and scary.

Elizabeth started to back away from him in the direction of the stockroom when the stranger spoke again.

"Don't run, child." As the figure spoke, he reached into his jacket and drew out what looked like a large sword.

For an instant, Elizabeth tried to grasp how such a large sword could possibly fit under his jacket but stopped moving toward the stockroom. Anne was in there and this man could hurt her.

He smiled cruelly and, still staring down at her, said, "Your death may finally trigger his return, child. None of the others have but you are special somehow. Unique. Some other line runs in your blood I cannot quite make out. No matter."

The man brought his sword back to swing it.

"It will soon be over."

"No!" Anne screamed as she appeared suddenly and launched herself into Elizabeth, knocking them both to the floor, just as the sword barely missed.

Her aunt hit her head as they crashed into a display box of America's Finest cigarettes.

The stranger had also hit a couple of racks hanging on the walls that tangled up his sword.

His large size was rather ill-suited for such a small space, but he pulled the sword loose and started around the corner of the display case to finish what he had started.

Elizabeth opened her mouth to scream not to hurt her aunt when a hand reached out and pulled her into the small room that had been her uncle's office.

She spun around to see an older man dressed like he had just came out of the 30's holding a cane. He was the one dragging her away from the attacker.

"Let go of me! My aunt is in there!" she screamed.

The man replied "He doesn't care about her. It's you he wants.

"Now, my name is John Watson and if you want to live, you are going to have to trust me!"

Elizabeth nodded her head just as the archway exploded and the door splintered as the massive sword hacked into it from without.

Both Elizabeth and John backed against an old metal desk. The older man stumbled but Elizabeth was able to stand as they backed away from the strange man who seemed to be growing and changing.

Growing in size and changing into a large dark knight like the ones she had seen in her story books. The top of his head nearly reached the ceiling. He grabbed the display case and threw it to the side of the room so he could reach her.

The hole in the wall was smoking and the smell of burning cigars was all around them, almost reminding her of her uncle George. But there was something else. That smell like the ragged man she had ran into earlier. Rot. Evil.

She looked straight up at him, defiant, her fear set aside. As if this one little girl was going to be able to stop a giant sword-wielding knight.

"Are you the rag man from this morning?"

The man spat, insulted, "No, girl, the hounds only seek out the bloodlines. I extinguish them."

He raised his sword to finish the job. Elizabeth looked at her Aunt laying on the floor half-covered with boards and stuff and wondered if she was still alive. Or if she would live out the day due to this horrible man.

The old man who had just saved her lay on the floor of the office bleeding from his forehead and yelling for her to run.

The dark knight spoke, "Your line ends now, blood of the Pendragon."

Just as he raised his sword once more, another figure entered the room coming between her and the knight.

The figure was holding something, a gem that glowed as the sword came down. The room glowed brighter as the knight was sent flying backwards across the shop, shattering the front window and landing on the sidewalk outside.

The new figure turned to her. "Elizabeth are you alright?" he asked.

She shook her head yes, still in shock. She was expecting another attack, but the evil man was nowhere in sight.

"John how are you?" said the new figure, a tallish man himself.

"Just bumped my head a little. Nothing to worry about." the man replied as he struggled to pull himself up.

"Well then, John, we must move quickly. The beast will be back as soon as the magic replenishes, and with that one it won't take long. Attend to Anne and get her to the limo in the back alley."

"Yes, of course," Watson replied as he stumbled through the wreckage of the door to kneel beside Anne. To Elizabeth's relief, she stirred.

The man holding the gem knelt down to Elizabeth's eye level. "You're going to have to trust me if you and your Aunt are going to survive, yes?"

Without hesitation, Elizabeth answered with a yes, then stared at the man as if he were suddenly familiar.

"Great-Granddad?"she said, confused.

He smiled and grabbed her hand. "Great-great-actually, but that memory of yours is going to take you places in the days ahead, little snowflake."

Outside the back of the shop the man named John Watson was helping Anne into a large car. Great Granddad bent down beside her.

"This might be difficult to understand but that creature in there was and is evil personified. And believe it or not, his mother is much worse. They won't stop until they have you." He then pulled something from his pocket. Her red ornament.

"I need you to do me a favor." He then broke the ornament.

She cried out, 'No," but it was too late.

He pulled out the silver snowflake that hung inside and inserted a silver chain to make a beautiful necklace.

"Elizabeth, I need you to never take this off. It has special powers that will help protect and hide you from those trying to find you."

"But you found me."

He smiled, tenderly, "Yes, well, you were never truly lost from me. Nor will you ever be."

"Now, your uncle John Watson there is going to take you and your aunt away from here. You have to understand that now that they know about you, the beast's mother won't stop until she finds you again."

"So, to protect you and your aunt you must always wear this charm. Do you understand?"

Elizabeth nodded slowly, sadly.

"Good. Now, go quickly." William looked to his old friend. "Go, John, to where we discussed. They have to disappear. I'll catch up with you soon."

He motioned for Elizabeth to get into the car but she stopped.

"My book!"

He smiled and held out her early Christmas present. "This one?"

She clutched it close as she stared at the home she was leaving behind and the grandfather she barely remembered from old photos who had just saved her and her aunt.

Looking at the title, he said, "There are some mighty good tales in there. A certain detective and his friend make it all worth the reading, I think."

"Great-granddad, please be careful."

He smiled "Without a doubt I shall, little snowflake, now you must go. I must make sure you aren't followed. Pity about the shop; it's where I've always bought my pipes of late."

The two older men nodded at one another and John hustled Elizabeth into the car and told the driver to go and go quickly.

Anne moaned as John pressed a cloth to her head, never minding he was bleeding himself.

Elizabeth took her aunt's hand in hers and looked at him. "Where will we go?"

"Somewhere safe. Now, don't you worry."

She clambered onto the back seat and watched as her old life retreated into memory.

"Uncle Watson, do you think we can stop somewhere and get a Christmas Cake?"

Watson smiled.

"I think that could be arranged. Merry Christmas, Elizabeth."

The girl slumped down into the seat, took her aunt's hand in hers, the book she'd received clutched to her chest, and looked at the man opposite her.

"Merry Christmas, Uncle John," she said. "Merry Merry Christmas."

###

next…

Camelot Forever
Pendragon's Return

by

Robert W. Hickey

Bill Nichols

2022

ROBERT W. HICKEY

CAMELOT FOREVER: LANCELOT'S REDEMPTION is the first novel written by Robert and in collaboration with Bill Nichols, but he's been around publishing a long time.

Robert has worked in the comic book industry, in several different aspects, for many years.

Robert and his brother Mike started Blue Line Art, the company that prints borders on comic art boards used by many professional artists and publishers in the comic industry.

Not happy with only supplying artists with paper Blue Line created bluelinepro.com, an online art store focused on offering art supplies specifically for the comic book artist.

He next created Sketch Magazine, a periodical that offers professional tutorials on every aspect of comic book creation and has been acting publisher from its inception.

Even before Blue Line, Robert had his hand in creating comic books. His projects ranged from time-traveling agents to superheroes and, most recently, following the adventures of a child with learning differences. Robert has over 12 properties currently in development for comics, online web comics and merchandise.

Outside of publishing Robert and his partners has opened a successful video game store (more here www.nostalgicvideogames.com).

Interests....

Spending as much times as possible with his wife Katie.

A longtime comic book reader, Robert keeps up with the latest Marvel Mutant battles and whichever earth the guy in blue tights is having his current adventure. He also enjoys watching Cincinnati Reds baseball, Cincinnati Bengals football and University of Kentucky basketball.

Follow Robert at http://www.robertwhicky.com for information on future releases, blogs, and other projects.

Bill Nichols

Bill is a longtime comic book writer, inker and editor with a projects board that won't ever be empty, even as the published list gets longer. He is the senior editor for Sketch Magazine. He has worked on comics such as Blood & Roses, StormQuest, as well as his own Sparta Bay imprint.

Published by Robert W. Hickey at Amazon.

This eBook is licensed for your personal enjoyment only. This ebook may not be re-sold or given away to other people. If you would like to share this book with another person, please purchase an additional copy for each recipient. If you're reading this book and did not purchase it, or it was not purchased for your use only then please return to your favorite ebook retailer and purchase your own copy. Thank you for respecting the hard work of these authors.

Made in the USA
Las Vegas, NV
17 September 2021

30534496R00171